my not so
Super Sweet life

Cat Crawford just wants to be normal—or at least as normal as a daughter of Hollywood royalty can be. And it looks like fate is granting her wish: she's got an amazing boyfriend, Lucas; her fabulous cousin, Alessandra, living with her; and her dad planning his second marriage to a great future stepmom. That is, until her prodigal mother reveals on national television that she has something important to tell her daughter…causing a media frenzy.

Lucas Capelli knows his fate is to be with Cat, and he's worked hard to win her over once and for all. Unfortunately, Lucas has his own issues to deal with, including a scandal that could take him away from the first place he's truly belonged.

As secrets are revealed, rumors explode, and the world watches, Cat and Lucas discover it's not fate they have to fight if they want to stay together…this time, it's their own insecurities.

Well, and the stalkerazzi.

my not so
Super Sweet life

rachel harris

Entangled Publishing, LLC
2614 South Timberline Road
Suite 109
Fort Collins, CO 80525
Visit our website at www.entangledpublishing.com.

Edited by Stacy Abrams
Cover design by Alexandra Shostak

ISBN   978-1-50055-273-2

Manufactured in the United States of America

First Edition April 2014

To all the readers who have followed Cat's journey from the beginning…thank you. This story is my gift to you. Thank you for an amazing ride!

So Much for Normal

·Cat·

Once upon a time (say, like, four months ago), the phrase *girl bonding* was a foreign concept. An expression I never expected to say, or even think, without gagging. But not only am I not choking on the delicious, gooey, calorie-laden brownie I'm currently devouring, but a goopy green mask is in place, Hello Kitty slippers are on my feet, and I totally just snorted.

Welcome to my new normal.

As my very-soon-to-be-stepmother Jenna teaches, or rather, attempts to teach my uber-conservative cousin and rhythmically challenged best friend to do the running man, I marvel at how much my life has changed. This time last year, I would've scoffed at anything girly. I'd never been kissed—or even on a date. I had major trust issues, and my best friend was my *dad*. Now, I have a hot, swoonalicious boyfriend. I have not one but two close friends. And after sixteen and a half years of Mama drama, scandal-hungry paparazzi, and bizarre time-traveling escapades—thanks to my favorite gypsy girl Reyna—it looks as though I'm finally, maybe, *hopefully* getting a taste of normalcy.

So why does it feels like the other shoe is about to drop?

The sofa cushion dips, and a *whoosh* of air fans my face, yanking me from my tilt-a-whirl thoughts. Alessandra, my sixteenth-century ancestor, blows out a breath, her freshly scrubbed cheeks pink from exhaustion. I lift my lips in a smile and accidently crack my goopy mask in the process.

"You've got some moves, girlfriend," I say, nudging her with my elbow, not surprised. While my dancing left much to be desired during my jaunt to the past, Less had skills. Evidently, that particular talent carried over when she came to the future. Lowering my voice so Jenna and Hayley won't hear, I say, "All that complicated mumbo jumbo in packed ballrooms must've paid off. Too bad Austin's not here to see you shake your groove thang."

As with any other time I mention the boy's name, a dopey smile zips across my cousin's face. She's so whipped.

"It *is* a shame he is not here, but if he were, I doubt I would be dancing." Her dark eyes shine with humor. "I may be bolder than when I first arrived, but I'm a far cry from crazy."

She playfully lifts a waxed eyebrow, and my mask-cracked grin widens. Alessandra's easy use of modern lingo still amazes me. Her transition into a twenty-first-century teen has been almost effortless. Sure, she stumbled in the beginning, but now she's in the zone. Less is in love, starring in the school play, and fending offers from Hollywood, thanks to her fabulous stint in the Shakespeare Winter Workshop. It's as if she were born for this century, this life, and was simply biding her time in the Renaissance until a bit of gypsy magic made it all happen.

A twinge of envy pricks behind my ribs.

I'm happy for my cousin. I am. It's just…she's only been in my world for six weeks. She's found her place. Maybe it's about time I found mine.

My best friend Hayley plops onto the love seat across from me, snagging a brownie on her way down. "Must have chocolate," she says, breaking off a large chunk. She shoves it in her mouth, and her eyes roll back in bliss. "So good," she mumbles.

"Yeah, yeah, rub it in." Jenna frowns at the tray of calorific goodness. "You skinny misses pig out to your heart's content. I can take it, even if it *is* my bachelorette party."

Today's a teacher in-service day at school, which means the students have a mini-vacay. With Jenna's wedding on the horizon, what better way to spend the day than with bachelorette-inspired girly-time makeovers?

See? I'm totally evolving.

Licking her index finger, Jenna presses it into the scattered crumbs on the plate and then lifts it to her nose. She inhales audibly before heaving a dramatic sigh. "Two more days," she proclaims, wiping her finger on a napkin. "Two more days of rabbit food so I can fit into my dress, and then I'm wolfing an entire layer of wedding cake myself. Mark my words, girls."

Hayley picks up the television remote and powers on the mounted flat screen. "Hang in there, Miss J. It'll all be worth it when you see the pictures. Your dress is flipping fabulous."

Hayley is an aspiring fashion designer, so she'd know. She's also a fellow art nerd on the fringes of Roosevelt Academy's social order, and we became friends fresh from my jaunt to the past. Her mantra of *Keep Calm, Love Fashion* has been amusing me ever since. Her stamp of approval is like a thumbs-up from the fearsome Joan and Melissa Rivers, and it's as close as Jenna will ever get, since *that* particular duo won't be weighing in.

The details of Dad's wedding are super hush-hush, with only the inner circle even knowing the date. Tabloids have speculated for months. April in Catalina or June in Malibu; I've even heard October in Paris or Rome. The paparazzi will never guess an award-winning Hollywood director and the leading party planner of Beverly Hills are getting hitched in their own backyard, with a slim guest list of fifty, on Valentine's Day weekend.

"And speaking of fabulous…" Hayley selects *The Kate Lyons Show* from the menu. "I have such a clothing crush on this woman." Hugging a throw pillow close to her chest, she settles in to watch the program, tossing Jenna a defeated look. "No chance she'll be there, huh?"

Understandably, the wedding—and its noticeable lack of invited celebs—has been the topic du jour.

Jenna shakes her head. "Nope. Inviting her or anyone else in the media would've been like asking vultures to camp outside our front door. Peter and I want to keep this as low-key and off the radar as possible. We've seen the weddings with paparazzi stalking the family, following the kids to school." She shudders, and the smooth skin around her bright eyes tightens. "That's not happening to Cat."

Her tone is intense, proving what I've suspected all along — I'm the reason for the small wedding. True, Dad has never been into the trappings of his Hollywood status, and Jenna isn't the attention-getter I once pegged her to be. But this is their *wedding*. Dad's first marriage was over before it even began, and it certainly hadn't been rooted in love. Not the kind he has with Jenna, anyway. And Jenna's the ultimate girly-girl. If it weren't for me, and worrying about my safety, I know she'd have wanted a grand affair.

"It's not too late to change your mind," I tell her, for what has to be the hundredth time. "Money makes the world go round. You can easily get a new, snazzy location if you throw enough around, and as for the camera-toting vermin, I've dealt with them my entire life. I can handle it."

Jenna reaches over and takes my hand. "I know you can, Cat, but that's not the point. The three of us are finally becoming a family. That's what is important here, not impressing the world with glamour. For whatever reason, Caterina's been lying low lately, and your father and I don't want to tempt fate. Or give the media extra incentive to bother us."

She says *us*, but she means *me*. Nodding, I squeeze her hand. I understand where she's coming from, even if it does make me feel guilty. But Jenna is right about one thing. Caterina — my mother — *has* been quiet lately. Uncharacteristically so. And while I should be grateful for the lack of mortification, her silence only makes me anxious. You know what they say about the calm before the storm...

Pushing to my feet, I sigh and then walk toward the hallway, ready to wash the gunk off my face. By now, my skin should be officially exfoliated and smoother than a baby's butt. I've taken exactly two and a half steps when Kate Lyons's perky voice fills the room.

"Welcome back, everyone! And you're gonna be *so* glad you tuned in. My next guest has starred in tons of blockbusters such as *The Event Planner, Secrets and Vines,* and *No One Has to Know.*"

My feet freeze.

Here comes the storm.

"And she's here today with a startling revelation," the woman continues, shooting ice down my back. "Please join me in welcoming Caterina Angeli!"

My birth mother's name attached to the phrase "startling revelation" is not a good sign.

But it's like a car wreck. I can't *not* look. I can't not turn back. I backpedal to the living room, the sound of my pounding pulse almost eclipsing the studio audience's enthusiastic applause. I fall in a heap in front of the television and watch as the woman who gave me life, the woman I haven't seen in person in more than ten years, graces the New York City soundstage. My boyfriend Lucas wonders why my first response is to push people away when there's trouble, why I'm so sure that he'll leave me one day.

This woman is the reason.

A gentle hand takes mine, and without looking, I know it's Alessandra. She must be dumbstruck. I was when I saw *her* mom back in the sixteenth century. The two women are doppelgangers—those tend to run rampant around me—but the resemblance stops at appearance. Personality-wise, they couldn't be more different. My aunt is actually a lot like Jenna, a blessing and a curse for my cousin. I know Less is happy with her choice to stay in the future, but she misses her mother terribly. Seeing mine, as horrid as she is, must suck an egg. I squeeze back to say I'm here and tug my knees to my chest.

"Thanks so much for having me, Kate," my mother says, trademark wide smile in place as she turns to the audience and waves.

She's as polished and beautiful as ever. Long, dark hair shining under the lights, dark smoky eyes made up to perfection. People always say we look alike. In some ways we do—we've got the same hair color and eyes, and according to Wikipedia, around the same height. But the wide smile that's launched a hundred lipsticks looks completely wrong on my smaller face. The graceful beauty Caterina Angeli is known for just isn't happening; I don't have a team of touch-up professionals at my beck and call. And as for that air of natural confidence my mother exudes, despite what people may think, all I've done is perfected the art of faking aloofness. I'm the non-airbrushed, unpolished, slightly awkward version of the temptress of Hollywood. Yay, me.

"Thank you all for such a warm welcome," my mother says. "It really means a lot." Manicured, clasped hands fly to her chest as her mouth closes in a gentler (though no less fake) smile. What looks to be tears rush to her eyes, and I roll mine as she says, "It feels so good to be among friends again."

Among friends? Is she referring to the nameless sea of admiring strangers or the glamazon talk show host with dollar signs for eyes? And as for *again,* she's only been out of the public eye for a nanosec. A couple months max. Jenna sinks beside me, her disbelieving snort hinting at thoughts aligned with mine.

Ms. Lyons leans closer in her padded chair, face pulled in concern. "Are you okay?" she asks, grabbing the nearby tissue box. I'm sure she's thinking, *Please cry. That'll skyrocket my ratings.*

Mommy Dearest nods, making a production of plucking several tissues from the box. "Thank you, Kate." She takes a breath and looks back at the audience. "You know, celebrities aren't perfect. We make mistakes. *I* make a lot of them—but you know that. You watch *TMZ*."

She winks, like the scandals and liaisons that have haunted me my entire life are no big deal, and the dumb crowd chuckles.

Kate shakes her head. "We know most of that is exaggerated."

"You're right," my mother agrees. "But no one's ever confused me with a saint. I've singlehandedly kept the tabloids in print. Even they'd tell you, though, that I've changed. I'm getting older. And more than anything, I'd like to fix some of my past mistakes."

Jenna's body goes still beside me. That's my first hint that trouble is coming.

Then Caterina looks into the camera, almost as if she can see straight through it, directly at me. My *second* warning. "I have a beautiful daughter," she says, and the world around me ceases to exist. "She's named after me, as everyone knows, but we're not close. Haven't been for some time. That's my fault, and it's the biggest regret of my life."

Tears fall down her flawless, olive-toned cheeks, but I'm a statue. A hunk of emotionless marble, like the kind Lucas uses in his art. My mother, the internationally famous actress

Caterina Angeli, is on television, admitting to the world how she's failed me. And I've got nothing. No tears, no anger, no raining down of disbelieving curses. Nothing.

"I miss my daughter, Kate," she says, closing her eyes as mine widen. Alessandra shifts closer and slings an arm around my back. "I have something I need to tell her. Something important that must be said in person." She pauses to draw a breath, and in that brief moment, I just *know* my life is about to change forever.

She nods as if agreeing with my assessment and announces, "That's why I'm attending Peter's wedding this weekend in Beverly Hills."

Hayley makes a noise that sounds like a teakettle on crack. Alessandra's hold crushes my lungs. As for Jenna, if it's possible to look both terrified and pissed at the same time, that's her. Nostrils flared, color gone, jaw clenched and shaking. Phones immediately start ringing. Soon, those vultures will be circling our door. The cat's out of the bag.

So much for my normal.

"Caterina Angeli does it again," I whisper.

It's My Life

·Lucas·

Dad's home. His voice rumbles from down the hall as I drop my gym bag on the ground. I want to take a shower, call my girl, and crash—but he's here. For two weeks it's been building, the need to tell him I'm done. That soccer isn't for me, and *I'm* not David. I know he's gonna freak. Then be silently pissed and distant. He might even shut down again. But I can't let that stop me. I can't keep living someone else's life. This has to happen, and after the beat down Coach just put us through on our so-called holiday, I'm ready for it to be today.

I kick off my sneakers in the mudroom, an asinine thought crossing my mind. Maybe his being here early is a sign. A month ago, I'd have called myself an idiot for thinking it. Supernatural crap is for losers and people with too much time on their hands, or so I thought before I met Cat's cousin. Or saw the gypsy Reyna with my own eyes. Now, I don't know what to think, but I know that divine intervention or not, I'm getting this over with.

Endorphins pound my veins as I walk down the hall, gilded frames lining both sides. School photos, family portraits, my big brother playing sports. The shrine of David, I call it. I stop in front of the last one, putting off the inevitable for another minute, and stare at him from back when he was around my age, kicking ass and taking names for his team in San Diego. They won that day, thanks to that goal. It's also the last one he ever scored.

My big brother was a hero. Not just because I looked up to him, and not even because he was incredible on the field. David actually saved a woman's life. He stepped in when a bunch of thugs were jumping her outside his apartment complex late one night. Unfortunately, it meant they turned on him instead.

Swiping the sweat and grime from my face with the hem of my shirt, I think through my plan again. Get in. State the facts. Get out.

Dad will respect honesty.

I tap my fist against the frame.

Or he'll have a complete breakdown, and it will be all my fault.

When I finally step into the living room, conflicted but resolved, my younger sister looks up from the TV.

"Dad's home." Angela's voice sounds off. She's sprawled out on the sofa, flipping through channels like David Beckham running down the wing. Her bare foot taps the leather cushion, and the remote bounces in her hand. She's anxious. Or upset. And that can only mean one thing.

"They're at it again?" I ask, parking my ass on the edge of the sofa.

Angela's frown silently answers my question.

Our parents don't have knock-down, drag-out fights or anything. In fact, they don't argue at all. That would require emotion from Dad, and since David died, that's something he doesn't have. As for Mom, her general M.O. is not to rock the boat. To keep everyone happy and hold us so close we suffocate. But lately things have been weird. Dad's schedule has been erratic, Mom's rosary rarely leaves her fingers, and they've both been talking in code. Dad's business partner has been calling a lot, so I figure it must be about the record label. But if something happened to make Angela this stressed, maybe I should hold off on talking to Dad.

"You don't think we're moving again, do you?"

Her question yanks me from staring a hole through the closed office door. My jaw pops as pieces of the puzzle start to click. *Oh, hell no*. Moving isn't an option.

"My sweet sixteen is in a few weeks," she continues, shoving a thick section of dark hair behind her ear. "I'm *finally* getting invited to parties. Yesterday, Desiree and Ciara saved me a seat in the cafeteria, and Micah smiled at me in gym." I'm wracking my brain trying to remember who this Micah is when Angela's big brown eyes find mine. "We only just got here, Luc. I don't want to go back."

"We're not going anywhere," I promise. The panic in her eyes starts to recede, and I squeeze her painted toes for reassurance. "I don't care what it takes. I'll play soccer for the rest of my life if I have to, but we're not leaving. We're for damn sure not going halfway across the world."

My family moves more often than not. A constant back and forth between the States and Italy, where Dad grew up and where the home base for Lirica Records is. Four years ago when he transferred to the Milan office permanently, neither of us cared. Leaving our house in L.A.—the backyard where David had just taught me passing drills—was easy. The life and friends that I'd made had been dispensable.

It was during the last move to Italy that I became the soccer star. Not so much because I wanted to, but because it's what Dad needed. Grief makes life lose its color, and his was muted gray…until I stepped into my brother's cleats. Soccer was always David's sport, his and my dad's, and giving it back to Dad seemed like the least I could do. For a while, it helped us both.

Being on the team shot me into the in-crowd. I went from being the quiet kid, shaping clay, to the guy with tons of connections. Soccer gave me a life and friends. But it wasn't *my* life. And those so-called friends were fake as shit. All they cared about was how many goals I scored on the field and how many girls I went through when I was off. But here, I have real friends. And I only want one girl.

I'm not leaving Cat. Dad will have to snap out of it and fight me first.

Like my thoughts conjure him, the door to the office opens. Mom bustles out, her bottom lip trapped between her teeth, and Angela springs up on the sofa.

"Everything okay?" my sister asks.

Mom's gaze collides with mine, and guilt, worry, and a dozen other emotions I can't name flash on her face. The exact opposite of Dad, who strolls in behind her, lifeless as ever.

"Right as rain," he answers. The stupid phrase is as fake as his detached tone of voice. He's a shell of the man I once knew. Dad used to be funny as hell and laugh all the time. He used to fit the stereotype of the hotheaded Italian, impatient and stubborn. *Used to.* Dull gray eyes focus on me, and a brief flicker of emotion passes as he asks, "How was practice?"

"Good, sir." It's my standard, automatic reply. If I told him the truth—that I hated every second, and would rather be sculpting in the studio or tinkering under the hood of a car—who knows what he'd do.

But then I remember my decision.

Cracking my knuckles, I go back over my canned speech. Soccer doesn't make me happy. We can still watch a match together or play one-on-one, but I'm quitting the team. Screw the championship, the scouts, and their supposed scholarships. We don't need the handout. Even if we did, Mr. Scott says I can get one easily for art. But that's a whole other issue.

Dad snatches the newspaper on the way to his recliner. Another minute and he'll be lost in world politics, finance, and sports. Anything to keep his brain busy and away from home.

It's now or never.

I push to my feet and walk forward until I'm standing in front of him. My throat feels thick as I rub my hands down the sides of my shorts and stare at his bowed head of thick, graying hair. "Dad, you got a minute? I want to talk to you about the team."

He doesn't react right away. Just turns another damn page. But from behind me, I hear Mom exhale audibly, and

I know she's reciting a string of prayers in her head. She knows how I feel. That I want to major in studio art, not business, and get a Fine Arts degree. She's supportive—to an extent. She just doesn't speak up. She doesn't say anything when Dad pushes about games or my future at the label, and in a way, I can't blame her. This isn't her battle to fight. It's mine.

I scratch the back of my head, undecided if it makes it easier or harder that he hasn't looked up. "The team's great," I say, clasping my hands behind my neck. "Coach knows his stuff, and he's tough as nails. Today was supposed to be a student holiday, but he had us in for extra hours, and I respect it." At this point I realize I'm stalling. Rambling and talking out of my ass. I exhale, frustrated, and say, "Look, Dad, I just don't—"

"David's coach at USD was tough, too," he interrupts. "It's good for you. Character building. It'll prepare you for college." He folds the newspaper in half, gaze now glued to the sports section.

The double whammy of comparing me to my brother and dismissing me so easily punches me in the gut. I don't know why it continues to surprise me. Hurt me. You'd think I'd be used to it.

My unclasped hands smack against my thighs, and a small thrill of satisfaction jolts through me when my father jumps. He raises his head, an actual emotion—confusion—swirling in his eyes. I open my mouth and say, "You're not listening to me. This isn't about Coach. I'm trying to tell you that I—"

"Lucas, you'd better come see this."

In the second it takes me to glance over, Dad lowers his

head again to the paper. I curse under my breath. "Angela, what the hell?"

Mom pops me on the back of the head, and I feel like crap when I see my sister's torn face, but damn. She knows better than anyone how important this conversation is. How rare it is to get Dad's full attention. How close I just came to finally ending it.

"Sorry." Gnawing her lip, Angela lifts her chin toward the television on the other side of the room. "But I thought you'd want to know what was happening."

I look over to see what could possibly be so huge that she had to interrupt us, and it takes me less than two seconds to understand.

A beautiful brunette is on the screen, her face tear-streaked and Botoxed. Everyone in the world knows who Caterina Angeli is, the rumors and scandals that follow her. But only a select few know how she destroyed the girl I care about. And that it's because of this woman that she sometimes still pushes me away.

The obnoxiously perky host glances at the spellbound crowd. "*This* weekend, you say?"

Cat's mom nods and dabs her eyes as she says, "I only hope my daughter accepts my apology."

I'm halfway to my room, cell phone in hand, before I even know what I'm doing. The showdown with Dad can wait. My girl needs me.

Alessandra answers her phone on the third ring, and I say, "I'm on my way."

The Shoe Drop

·Cat·

Our cell phones haven't stopped. Calls and text messages have been incessant, long-lost friends and acquaintances coming out of the freaking woodwork. Dad's crack security team arrived a little while ago and at least put the beat down on the constant *ding-dong* of the doorbell, but even they can't drown out the noise. The *click* of cameras, the hum of voices—the sound of the other shoe not just dropping, but drop*kicking*.

It would appear that normal in this town is as mythical as happily ever after.

Outside my window, neighbors crowd the streets filled with paparazzi. It's amazing how quickly people will sell you out for five measly minutes of fame. Hock your deepest secrets to the highest bidder. I guess if fame isn't shoved down your throat since birth, it's hard to see how fleeting and superficial it all is. How isolating and lonely. But since Jenna and I have *slightly* more pressing concerns today than teaching life lessons or divulging juicy tidbits, our poor neighbors are left storyless, in turn leaving the vile shutterbugs with nothing more to go on than shot after shot of our fascinating front door.

It serves those bloodsuckers right.

Justin Timberlake serenades the living room again, and Jenna lurches for her phone. I don't have to see the screen to know it's Dad. He's spitting fire and stuck in gridlock, and in lieu of misguided road rage, he's been blowing up our cell phones every few minutes.

"Peter, we can't get married like this." Jenna is borderline hysterical. Her constant pacing halts as she lifts a slat of the closed blinds, then drops it like the vermin outside are contagious. "My parents won't be able to make it down the street." She thumps her head against the wall and mutters, "That selfish witch ruined my wedding."

I suck air between my teeth, imagining Dad's reaction. He's totally blaming himself. Apparently, in a horribly ill-advised attempt to make peace with my birth mother, Dad sent her a wedding invitation via her agent. It was common courtesy, he said, and he'd assumed the gesture would go unanswered.

Obviously, that plan backfired spectacularly.

Alessandra rests her head against mine. "Lucas is on his way."

This is the third time she's said this in the last twenty minutes. Lucas called right after Caterina dropped her bombshell, while I was still in a *what-the-heck-just-happened*

coma. I don't know how he knew that I needed him. If my
Italian hottie shares Hayley's talk TV obsession, it's certainly
news to me. But at this point, I don't care. I'm just glad he's
coming.

Learning to lean on Lucas has definitely been a transition.
I'm so used to being the strong one in any situation, never
showing anyone how much things affect me. But I'm slowly
figuring out how to let go. To let him in. To trust that Lucas
has me.

At least for now…

I whisk away the cruel taunt whispered in a voice way
too much like my mother's and glance at the remains of our
aborted bachelorette party. When the latest installment in
the Crawford/Angeli family drama reared its hideous head,
and the bride-to-be got demoted to phone duty, our driver
took Hayley home. As for Less and me, we haven't budged
from our spots in the living room, other than to finally wash
the gunk off my face. (If tabloids ever got a pic of me like
that, it'd definitely make the front cover, right under the
headline *Vixen's Daughter Is Really an Alien.*) I guess it's
possible Alessandra's still in shock over seeing her mother's
doppelganger on screen—but from her constant state of
fidgety, I'd say *I'm* the bigger concern here.

I know what she's thinking. What they're *all* thinking.
They're waiting for me to freak. To go nuts, lose my bananas,
and declare I'm taking off for a commune. A person doesn't
go ten years without any semblance of contact from her
estranged mother only to sit mute when something like this
happens.

But the truth? I'm not silently freaking. I mean, yeah,
I *am* angry she 'fessed up to her sucky parenting skills on

national television. It annoys the ever-loving snot out of me that she used this admission for her own gain—I don't doubt for a second that she made a buck out of today's appearance. And it *is* total crap that she sold out Dad and leaked the details of his and Jenna's wedding.

But…I'm also curious.

Is it so bad that a tiny, infinitesimal part of me hopes that maybe, *just maybe*, my mother meant what she said? That she misses me and actually wants to know me? I've spent most of my life believing that I wasn't good enough. That she viewed me through the lens of her impossibly high standards and found me lacking. The chance that I was wrong is like a drug. A dangerous, potent need roiling inside, begging for relief.

Jenna plops down beside me, her phone now in her lap. Linking her arm around mine, she says, "I just don't get Caterina's angle. What stunt could she be trying to pull now?" She purses her lips and after a moment, shakes her head. "Of course, your dad said she's not answering his calls. *No* surprise there."

It's been like this for the last half hour. Ever since my mother's segment ended and Jenna flipped off the television, the verbal tirade has been endless. Jostling my elbow, she asks, *again*, "How you holding up, sweets?"

"I'm fine," I say through clenched teeth. I know she hears the edge in my voice, but I can't help it.

Jenna has every right to be pissed about what happened—I sure as heck would be if my wedding were ruined. But the digs and slams against my mother, followed by the hovering hen act, is rapidly driving me batty.

I need to get out of here.

She shifts so she can better stare into my eyes. "Are you sure? You know you can scream or vent or talk it out if you want to. I'm here for you. We both are," she adds, nodding toward Less. "This has been a *crazy* day, and no one would judge you one bit for losing it. I'm certainly freaking." When I don't return her forced smile, she drops hers and sighs. "Listen, I don't know what that woman is planning, but I promise you this: she *won't* hurt you again."

Really, *really* need to get out of here.

"I know," I say, putting on the old familiar façade of confident indifference. "She can't hurt me again because I won't let her."

That much is at least true because I refuse to play her game. If my mother really does want to meet, then it'll be on my terms. It'll be a fact-finding mission, a bit of much-needed closure, plain and simple. If closure leads to more, such as an actual relationship, well…

The doorbell rings, breaking off my train of thought. My pulse rate accelerates as I push to my feet. I know who waits on the other side of the madness. Thank God he lives close. Alessandra and Jenna exchange a glance as I rush by, but I don't care. I shoot right past them, jogging to eat up the seemingly huge distance between the living room and my front door.

Lucas will make the panic in my blood go away. He'll remove the weird lump in my throat. Just looking into his eyes does that. I've stopped questioning why. It doesn't matter if divine intervention, an extremely odd coincidence, or simply Reyna being Reyna put Lucas in my path. What matters is that for the first time ever, at least in *this* century, a guy honestly cares about me, and not the Hollywood trappings.

In fact, Lucas seems to hate the whole scene even more than I do.

So when I finally reach the door, I don't hesitate. I don't care that a bazillion flashes are about to go off or that a picture of this meeting will end up on Perez Hilton. At least I won't be the green, cracked-mask-faced girl standing next to an Italian god. Releasing a relieved breath, I throw open the door, needing to look into those bottomless chocolate-brown eyes. They always reach into my soul, calming me. Well, interchangeably calming and exciting me.

As expected, flashes go off the second I stick my head outside. My fake smile holds as I face the onslaught and close the door. There's no way I'm going back in there. It takes a half second for Lucas to turn, but then he does, golden curls catching in the breeze and rich brown eyes locking with mine.

The only problem is they're *not* peaceful, as I'd expected. More like the exact opposite.

What the hay?

Mi Casa Es Su Casa

·Lucas·

Flashes explode behind me and reporters scream questions from the gate as I stare into the wildness of Cat's eyes.

I took too long.

My shower was the quickest in history. I sped the entire way here—if I could've taken my motorcycle, I would've gotten here even faster. But glimpsing the fear she's finally letting me see, I realize even that wouldn't have been fast enough.

"Baby, I'm so sorry." I pull her into my arms, picture-snapping asshats be damned. "That woman is a pyscho."

Instead of agreeing like I expect, Cat's entire body stiffens. A warning bell goes off in my head as I lean back and brush away strands of hair from her makeup-free face. I almost do a double take. Cat is easily the hottest girl I've ever met. She doesn't need all that junk. But she never goes anywhere without it. Hair, makeup, clothes—they're like her armor. A wall she throws up between her and the world. Protection against the very things happening around us right now, and without that mask, she looks more vulnerable. Every protective instinct I have goes on full-scale alert as my hands lock around her back.

"What's going on?"

It's a dumb question. Obviously, the entire world knows what's going on. Her mom sold her out on television, and jerkoffs with expensive cameras and cheap cologne are camped outside her front door. Security is here, too, enough to rival a damn One Direction concert, but it's her reaction in my arms that worries me. Her mother *is* a psycho, and she's caused enough problems in our relationship without being in her daughter's life. I can't imagine the havoc she'd cause if Cat lets her get a foot in the door.

She darts a glance behind me and subtly shakes her head. "I just need to get out of here. Take me?"

I don't hesitate. "Anywhere," I tell her.

Her shoulders visibly sag in relief, and I wait as she walks over to the head of security. When I first pulled up at the gate, the man made it seem like guarding Cat was a matter of national security. That I could appreciate, even if his attitude did terrify the crap out of me. But from here, I can tell Cat's not scared at all. The dude towers over her and is clearly not happy with her wanting to leave, but that doesn't stop her. One thing I've learned in the last couple months is that very few things do. There's just no arguing with Cat. Not when she's determined.

Sure enough, a minute later she ducks inside to yell

good-bye and then walks back toward me, the storm in her eyes beginning to fade.

"I promised Jack we'd be good," she says, jutting her thumb toward the mammoth standing behind her. "He won't smother me with surveillance, and we won't try to duck his tail."

The guy's biceps are larger than my head, and he has at least six inches on my five eleven. There's no way in hell I'd mess with this guy, but I'm glad to see her feistiness returning. "And where will he be following us?"

Cat surveys the crowd several feet away and purses her lips. "I'll tell you in the car."

My protective vibe gets a shot of adrenaline as we make our way to where I parked. Security succeeded in keeping the paparazzi off her property, but photographers surge the gate as we walk. A frenzy of camera clicks and questions follow each step we take.

"Are you going to see your mom?"

"What's the big secret?"

"Are you the maid of honor?"

"Have you met Kate Lyons?"

And my personal favorite: "You're just like your mom. Who's the boy toy?"

Through them all, Cat's mask of calm, cool collectedness never fails. I hate that look. It took me months to break through, and seeing it return is like a messed-up omen. My jaw clenches as a thrum of energy shoots through me. Soccer practice and my three-mile run earlier wore me out to the point of exhaustion—but right now, that feels like a lifetime ago.

I help her get in the car and then jog around the front,

slamming my door seconds later. My knuckles turn white as I grip the wheel. These people are taking a moment that is so personal, so *real,* for the girl I'm falling for, and throwing it back in her face like it's entertainment.

If they hurt her—if that *woman* hurts her—I can't be held responsible for my actions.

Cat curls her hand around my clenched fist and says, "I'm okay."

Her voice is soft, like she's talking me down off a ledge. My job today is to protect her, to take care of her, and yet somehow the roles got reversed. Releasing a breath, I look at her from the corner of my eye and flip my hand around so I can lift hers to my mouth. "You're amazing, you know that?"

A small smile plays on her lips. *I* put it there. A thrill of satisfaction clenches my chest, along with the feelings I have for this girl. They grow deeper every day. The anger, the adrenaline, they dissipate as we both take a breath and stare at each other. For a brief moment, it's just the two of us locked away in a bubble surrounded by chaos.

Then I press a kiss against her fingertips, inhale the scent of rose, and set her hand on my thigh. We need to get going before the paparazzi ruin everything again. I start the engine and ask, "Where to?"

"Just drive," she says, lowering the visor to hide her face. "Take a right at the stop sign, and I'll lead you from there."

Nodding, I glance in the rearview mirror at the photographers waiting for a shot. The gate slowly opens, and security steps in to prevent a mob attack. My stomach knots in disgust as I reverse.

The circle begins closing in the second I'm back on

Roxbury Drive. Screw not causing a scene. Revving my fine-tuned engine, I jerk forward like I'm gonna run them over, and chuckle when they jump back in fear. I'd never really do it, but they don't know that. And watching *them* cower for once feels damn good.

Hearing Cat laugh—a free, lighthearted sound that's worlds away from the haunted girl of a few minutes ago—feels even better.

Smiling for the cameras, hoping they can read the implied *"F-you"* in my eyes, I drive through the space my stunt provided and wave good-bye.

. . .

An hour later, I turn in to the gated entrance of the Michaels' beach house in Malibu. The place is sick. Hanging with Austin, you'd never know his family is loaded. Or that his dad is a senator with a stick up his ass. He's just your normal, surf-obsessed guy whipped by the girl he cares about—and that's a feeling I'm familiar with. I key the security code Cat rattles off and glance at her as the gate glides open.

"Why here?"

"Because it's not home," she replies, shifting her head against the seat to meet my gaze.

Since we left Beverly Hills, we haven't talked about her mom, our security tail, or the jerkoffs trailing them. We listened to music. We looked out over Pacific Coast Highway. We debated who'd kick whose ass in an artistic battle, Michelangelo or Chamberlain. I gave the battle to her, since she did *meet* the man during her trip to the past. And because I'm nothing if not chivalrous. But now that we're here, away from the madness, I need to know what's going on.

"And home's suddenly a bad thing?"

Cat sighs. "I needed a break from the drama. They mean well, it's just..." A line forms in the smooth skin between her eyes. "They don't understand. Look, Luc, I get it. What my mom did was wrong on a massive scale. But it's also the first time she's even acknowledged that I exist. She *totally* deserves Dad and Jenna hating on her," she admits before shrugging a shoulder. "But I just couldn't listen to it anymore."

I nod stiffly, jaw throbbing from holding back a response, and accelerate through the open gate.

I hear what she's saying. More, I understand what she's not. Cat has abandonment issues like you wouldn't believe, and it all stems from her mom. She split when Cat was five, and the only contact they've had since has been sharing the occasional tabloid cover. When Caterina Angeli goes nuts or falls face-first into another scandal, her daughter is the press's favorite target. Another reason I know the weeks ahead are going to suck.

But despite everything the woman's done, or I should say *hasn't* done, I sense her claws sinking in. It pisses me off. Too much time has passed for her to go Mom of the Year now. There has to be an end goal we're not seeing, and though I haven't figured it out yet, I will. We've fought too much—lookalike ancestor exes, gypsy magic, and Cat's own stubbornness—to let an attention-hungry, deceitful bitch take us down.

Nothing is going to hurt my girl. Not on my watch.

At the top of the hill, I park and get out, lifting my chin

at the security stationed at the bottom. Jack actually waves. Looking around the Michaels' estate, he probably figures it's a better option than Cat's house anyway. Her dad is the strangest Hollywood player I've ever heard of. According to *Forbes* magazine, they're rolling in money, but other than the high-price zip code and security gate, you'd never know it. They are ridiculously normal and low-key. He won't even let Cat on the back of my bike — at least not *yet*. I'm slowly wearing him down on that one.

"Does anyone know we're coming?" I ask, taking her hand.

Cat nods. "Yeah, Alessandra called Austin earlier."

Even though we're in a gated property on a private beach, I scan our surroundings as we walk to the front door. Manicured shrubs and thick trunks of towering trees give too much room for photographers to hide. Halfway to the entrance, I catch movement and automatically shift Cat behind me.

Austin strolls out the front door, wearing board shorts and flip-flops, hair wet as usual.

"Welcome to Casa de Michaels," he declares, arms slung wide. "This place has harbored many a scandalized politician, so you two miscreants should feel right at home."

He winks, and Cat shakes her head with a snort. Leave it to Austin to make light of a stressful situation. *Thank God.*

"You're such a dork," she says, but I hear the smile in her voice, and I send him a grateful nod.

Austin subtly returns it.

"Dork, charming prince, take your pick. I answer to them all." He grins as he tosses his keys in the air and catches them behind his back. "But a third wheel I'm not, so

I'm headed out. The door's unlocked, the kitchen is stocked, and the waves are killer. Help yourselves to anything, and hey, if you trash the place, even better."

Austin's smile is tight after he fires off the last remark. It's no secret that he and his old man are on the outs. For all my family's problems, at least Dad's not a complete ass. He'd never treat me or Angela the way Austin's father treats him. The Michaels family is a whole other level of dysfunction.

After keying a code in a side panel, Austin steps back and the garage door groans open. Sunlight streams in, my eyes adjust, and my jaw unhinges. Inside, parked next to his red truck, is a Ferrari Enzo.

"Hot damn."

Austin chuckles as I step forward, reverently skimming my fingertips over the body. The Enzo is rare. Only four hundred of them are even in existence. Made completely out of carbon fiber, this baby can go from zero to sixty in three point three seconds. It's a street legal racecar.

Stroking the tapered nose, I say, "What I wouldn't give to get under her hood." Cat elbows me in the ribs, and I tuck her back against my side. "Don't worry. I want to get under yours, too."

She rolls her eyes like I'm an idiot, but a smile twitches her lips.

"Man, go for it." I look back to see Austin shake his head in disgust. "It's only collecting dust anyway. Another one of my father's toys."

His eyes harden as he stares at the car, and I can tell he means it. My palms itch to accept…but that's not why we're here. We're here for Cat, and she's more important than a car. Even my *dream* car.

"Maybe some other time."

"You got it." Austin hops in his truck, guns the engine, and rolls down his window. Music pours out, and he raises his voice to say, "Seriously though, go wild in there. A cleaning crew comes every Friday to restock the place, so *mi casa es su casa,* all right?"

I press a kiss against Cat's hair, tightening my grip around her shoulder. "Thanks, man."

He nods. Transferring his attention to the girl in my arms, Austin's smirk drops as he reaches back to lower the music. "Cat, you know we've got this, right? You're part of Less's family, which means you're now part of mine. Between the three of us"—he tosses a glance in my direction—"we've got you covered. No one's gonna mess with you. You hear me?"

A small shudder rocks her frame, and an intense loathing of Kate Lyons floods my system. Cat squeezes my hand, somehow sensing my emotions, and says softly, "I do. Thanks, Austin. For being cool, and for letting us chill here for a while. I appreciate it."

I know that was big for her. It's been a process to accept help and to trust that people have her back. There's my silver lining in all this. Maybe she'll finally see that she's not alone.

Austin's normal smirk returns. "Hey, Alessandra called me a dashing hero, which I'm pretty sure is Shakespearean for awesome. Hooking you up scored me major points, so looks like we all win."

Cat laughs, and he winks. The truck inches forward, and we step back, watching as he drives down to the gate where security stops him. Apparently, the fact that this house is *his* doesn't matter; Jack subjects Austin to the same treatment I got earlier. Austin doesn't seem to care. With a good-natured shrug, he glances back at us with a smile, salutes Jack, and then hops back into his idling truck, apparently passing the inquisition. Thrusting his arm out the open window, he takes off, blaring music trailing behind him.

Silence falls, and we're alone.

Or, as alone as two teenagers can be with a large security detail several yards away. Cat sags against me, releasing a heavy breath, and I tighten my hold around her.

"What now?"

"Nothing," she says. "I don't want to do anything. I don't want to think, I don't want to talk. I just want to spend the rest of the day in ignorant bliss and pretend I'm someone else. *I'm* not the daughter of a Hollywood diva; *you're* not the son of a music mogul. Skeezy dudes aren't waiting to snap a picture of us making out or of me picking my nose. We're just a normal, everyday couple, with a huge, stinking house all to ourselves." She shifts her head back to give me an upside down grin. "But don't be getting any ideas. We're a *PG-13,* everyday couple with a house all to ourselves, you dig?"

Smiling, I touch my forehead to hers. "Have you seen PG-13 movies lately? I can definitely work with that rating."

Cat smacks the side of my thigh, but it's her genuine, full-body laugh that sends the sting. It's like an electric jolt straight to my chest. I would do anything for that sound. To keep that beautiful smile on her face and the fear out of her eyes. After years of feeling lost, moving back and forth across the world, I've finally found my home. This is where I belong.

And I'll do anything to protect what's mine.

Mood Kill

·Cat·

The lull of waves crashing on shore is every bit as magical as one of Reyna's tricks. If I could capture the tranquility in a painting or a photograph, I'd be famous. Or at least famous for something *good*. Closing my eyes, I listen to nature's symphony, feel the rhythmic rise and fall of Lucas's chest against my back, and it's almost easy to forget. Pretend we *are* just a normal couple, with no worries more pressing than bogus curfews, heinous exams, or possible onion breath. As for the last one, our dinner of frozen pizzas was thankfully onion-free, and we each popped a mint after scarfing it down. Any future lip-lock action will be minty fresh.

As if the onions would've stopped me anyway.

Turning in Lucas's arms, I shift my legs around his hips and clasp my hands around his neck. I realize I'm putting off the inevitable. In therapy-level denial that beyond this private beach, a world of chaos awaits. It'll be there tomorrow. Heck, it'll be there in an hour when we have to leave. But I'm not ready for reality yet. I want to lose myself in my boyfriend's kisses and tune out the endless questions circling my brain.

Lucas lifts an eyebrow, lowering his gaze to my mouth. "Can I help you?" he asks, shifting his hold to the small of my back. He tugs me closer, and my ankles lock behind him. "Is it PG-13 time?"

Despite everything, I smile, even as butterflies begin to swarm. Leaning forward, I whisper in his ear, "Yep. And if you're lucky, I'll even consider pushing that rating."

His breath hitches, a strangled sound caught between a groan and a chuckle, and a thrill of excitement passes through me. I love that I affect him so easily. It proves that he really *is* here just for me. That he's as into this thing between us as I am. I scoot back, watching as his chocolate eyes smolder, and my heart squeezes inside my chest.

I'll never get used to the way he looks at me.

Lucas believes I'm beautiful. The way his eyes both soften and blaze, the way he holds me in his arms. Solid, like he never wants to let me go. Strong, like I can always depend on him. Even though I know he's the beautiful one, Lucas makes me feel special. Cared for. *Wanted*.

Only one other guy ever did that, shot past my defenses and tipped my world on its axis. That was Lucas's Renaissance ancestor, Lorenzo. His sixteenth-century doppelganger was my first kiss—my first boy *anything*. He opened my heart during my time travel jaunt, taught me how to trust again, and more importantly, he gave me hope. Despite not knowing where I came from, or even who I really was, he got *me*. There's no denying that my time in the past with Lorenzo was nothing short of a fairy tale.

But being with Lucas in my *own* time? Being one hundred percent *myself*?

This is *real*. And it blows my ever-loving mind.

"Cat." Lucas whispers my name like it's precious. Like I'm worth something. And I so badly want to believe it. His blond curls catch in the breeze, gliding over the tanned skin on his forehead, and my fingers itch to tame them. To capture the silky locks and gently tug. He grins as if he can read my thoughts, and warmth floods my body, pooling in my stomach. Picking me up, Lucas lays me on a blanket of soft sand and says, "You have no idea what you do to me."

But I think I do. And that's what makes my head so wonderfully fuzzy.

That look is back in his eyes. Still smoldering, but soft now, too. The hint that his feelings are real…and deep. Before he can see the tears welling in mine, still unsure I deserve any of it, I clamp them shut and tug his head down.

"Make me forget," I beg him. It's a big step, admitting what I need, but this is Lucas. I know I'm safe. "I just want to forget everything but us right now."

His hand curls around the side of my face, tilting my chin as his thumb skims my throat. But he doesn't kiss me. He hovers, breathing me in until I reluctantly open my eyes. His gaze tracks over my face.

"We're all that matters." Our lips touch with each word he speaks, his stare so intense that I know he can see straight through to my soul.

Too many emotions clog my throat to reply, so I nod.

Right now, we're *everything*.

Lucas brushes his nose along mine, and my eyelids flutter. The last thing I see before they close completely is the dimple flashing in his cheek. Then his lips press into mine in a kiss meant to make the world fade away.

And it delivers.

Fingernails rake down my back, bringing a shiver. A low growl sounds in his throat, and I want to climb into his skin. Cologne, bodywash, something uniquely *him* fills my head, and when his tongue flicks out, licking the seam of my lips, I open eagerly, greedy for more.

The air around us is electric. Humming, vibrating, and heated, weighted with lust, desire, and even love. Yep, love. I'm falling for this boy, and that scares the crap out of me. But I can't give him up. I don't *want* to give him up.

When Lucas kisses me, nothing else matters. Time doesn't exist, our pasts don't matter, and my heart is unscathed. With every delicious nibble and each tender touch, he mends another broken shard, making me believe that one day I really can be normal. I trap his bottom lip between my teeth, and he groans, sinking his weight against me. Wrapping my arms around his back, I grip his shoulders so tight our bodies meld together. I never want him to stop.

Minutes…hours…days later, who knows, the sound of the real world breaks through the glorious haze. My cell phone is ringing. "Titanium" by David Guetta is my ringtone and current jam—fitting, since the lyrics pretty much describe my relationship with the paparazzi—but I *so* don't want to hear it right now. Hearing it means the end of Lucas's delicious kisses.

He raises his head, hair mussed and lips swollen, and I

really, *really* want to ignore it.

But I promised.

I gave Jack my word that I'd answer any calls and be ready to leave at the first hint of trouble. So even though I'd *much* rather continue our toe-tingling, drama-forgetting kisses that were just bordering on the good stuff…

"I have to get it," I say even as I tug Lucas back down for another one.

He chuckles low in his throat, balancing on his arms just enough to keep me from deepening it. I grumble when he evades me again, and he laughs aloud. God, he's got such a great laugh.

"Believe me," he says, his voice all kinds of husky and gravelly. *Sexy.* The notes of his Italian accent grow stronger when we're like this, sending a new batch of tingles skating down my body. "I could kiss you forever. But that security dude could rip my head off, so I'm thinking you should get it."

The firm muscles of his back bunch and flex beneath my hands as he reaches to grab my purse. He slides my phone from the side pocket and hands it over without glancing at the screen and then ducks to press an openmouthed kiss at the base of my throat.

"Make sure it's not important," he says, "and then we'll see what we can do about pushing that rating."

Oh, the boy is good; I'll give him that. "Well played, sir," I say, lifting my arm over my face. If it's anyone other than Jack, Jenna, Less, or Dad, I'm tossing this thing and tackling the smooth talker straddled above me.

With a lighthearted grin (an amazing feat that only Lucas could've accomplished today), I eye the screen…and immediately feel the smile drop from my face. The fine hairs on my arms lift, and the cool ocean air gliding over my skin feels arctic.

Sensing my shock, or perhaps feeling my entire body lock beneath him, Lucas leans back on his heels.

"Who is it?" His voice is still gravelly but now it has a distinct protective edge. I have a feeling that protective edge is about to explode.

Swallowing hard, I say, "Reality."

• • •

"How did *she* get your number?"

I grit my teeth, biting back a response to the way he emphasizes *she*. Obviously, Lucas is worried about me. He knows my past and is probably just as shocked as I am by my mother calling. At least, I *think* that's what I am. Shocked. Numb works, too.

"I don't know," I admit, sitting up and staring at my now-silent phone. I can't look away, my finger hovering over the home button as if the name will disappear if I look away or the screen goes black. "Guess Dad must've given it to her."

But that doesn't seem right, because if he did, surely he would've called and warned me. Tried to soften the blow before the author of every abandonment issue I have rocked my world. *Again.* The only other option, though, is that he gave it to her years ago…back when I got *hers*.

I still don't even know why I wanted it. Why I took it and programmed it in. I sure as heck never planned to use it. What would I have said? *"Hi, Mom, remember me? The fruit of your loins? The daughter you've ignored for eleven years? Feel like grabbing a movie some time?"*

Not a snowball's chance in Hades.

But I did take it. And programming it into my phone was like a morbidly reassuring link. Proof that if I absolutely *needed* to reach her—like if the world were ending or some other equally ungodly reason presented itself—I could.

Reassured was the exact opposite of how I felt, though, seeing her name flash on my screen. More like totally overwhelmed. Terror, confusion, anger, and hope all surged my body in a rush, scrambling my brain waves and knocking me utterly senseless.

I knew she planned to come. I should've expected her to reach out. But I don't think I possibly could've prepared for the reality of her actually doing it. A large part of me thought it was just another broken promise and scam.

As I continue to blink dumbly at the phone, "Titanium" begins again.

"Ignore it." Lucas closes his hand around mine, and I look away from *She-Devil mobile*. The same firm mouth that teased and kissed me into a giddy stupor a few moments ago is now set in a hard line. His blazing eyes are just as fierce. "Don't let that woman ruin anything else. This is *our* time. She can damn well wait."

A shiver racks my spine. I'm used to chill bumps when Lucas's accent gets deep like this. It means his emotions are running hot, and there's nothing more delicious than that voice whispering in my ear just before he licks it. But for the first time, my tremble is not from desire, but heartache.

"You don't get it." I can't keep the hurt and confusion out of my voice. Somehow, out of everything that's happened, Lucas not knowing why I need this surprises me the most. And considering the train wreck my life has become, that's saying something.

Jenna doesn't understand because she's all kindness and rainbows. She'd never treat someone the way my mom has. Dad's need to get all grouchy and Papa Bear makes total sense, too. It was always the two of us against the world, and dating Jenna hasn't lessened his Superman complex one iota. And as for Alessandra, well, her sweet, quiet fretting is par for the course. If the world worked according to *her* plan, everyone would get along, life would be one big hug-fest, and every child would grow up with the kind of parents she had. I know she'll support any decision I make, but she's totally going to worry herself into an ulcer while doing it.

But I thought if anyone were going to understand this, understand *me*, it would be Lucas.

"This isn't about *her*," I say, shaking my head as the phone continues to ring. "It has *never* been about her."

"What then?" His jaw ticks as he rakes his hand through his curls. "Why would you even think about hearing her out?"

The music stops, the call switching to voice mail. I let out a sigh, suddenly feeling exhausted. "Answers."

Looking away, I stare at the breaking surf. The *whir* of the roiling water and the crash of the swells match the turmoil that is my head.

"It's about finding out why she left us," I tell him. "Luc, that's all I've wanted to know since I was five years old. All I've cared about. And I think"—my dumb voice breaks, and I clear my throat to try again—"I think I deserve to find out."

Lucas doesn't respond. After taking a few deep breaths, I turn back, and his sympathetic gaze makes my chest ache. Tucking a strand of flyaway hair behind my ear, he palms my cheek and says, "Baby, you *do* deserve that. Hell, you deserve a mom who wouldn't have left you in the first place. But that's just it; we're not talking about another mom. We're talking about *yours*. And the thought of letting her hurt you again…" His Adam's apple bobs as he swallows. "It makes me want to bust something."

I love him for caring so deeply, but right now, there is another reason why I have to do this. If I want a real, all-in relationship with Lucas, the kind that Dad and Jenna have, heck, even the kind Alessandra and Austin have, then I need to be whole. My mom didn't just leave us when she took off years ago—she stole my self-worth and decimated any shot I had at true happiness. Until I hear *why*, my heart is never going to be fully open.

"The only way she can hurt me is if I let her." Climbing onto his lap, I wrap my arms around his neck and press a kiss to his lips. Seeing his worry does something to me. It feeds my soul and tells me I'm not alone. "But if I let this chance slip by, I'm always gonna wonder."

My phone beeps, indicating I have a message. Stupid, silly hope bubbles in my chest. I look up to see Lucas shake his head before resting it against mine. "Then I'm in. I hate it, but if this is something you have to do, then I'll be right there with you."

Relief floods my entire body. Finally, someone on my side. "That's all I need," I tell him, already hitting the play back button to hear my mother's message. I press a kiss against his lips and bring the phone to my ear. I know he's worried, but soon he'll see that I know what I'm doing. I'm in the driver's seat, *not* her, and everything is going to be totally fine.

Scratch that, it'll be better than fine, because in the end I'm going to find my *normal*.

Not on My Watch

·Lucas·

There's hope in Cat's eyes, and it kills me. The cameras swarming around us at LAX's baggage claim don't catch it, thanks to her dark sunglasses, but it's there. It entered while we were at the beach last night, and I saw it again when I picked her up this morning. The rest of her is calm and collected, the mask she puts on whenever she goes out in public. But the sparkle in her eyes, her slight squirms, and the gentle biting of her lip give her away. She's trying to hide her optimism from the stalkerazzi, but she's also hiding it from me. I hate *that* even more than the hope.

She thinks I don't get what she's going through. Why she needs to do this. But I do. She wants answers, closure. The same thing I want from Dad and wish I could have gotten with David. But what *she* doesn't get is that we're not dealing with a rational person. Caterina Angeli is a proven selfish manipulator who puts herself before her family. Anyone who's passed a supermarket tabloid or paid a second of attention to celebrity gossip knows that. For whatever reason, it doesn't seem to stick. People love her anyway and flock to her movies. But it doesn't change the fact that, from what I can tell, the woman gets off on treating others like trash, using and then tossing them aside, all to feed the crazy hype.

The hype that fuels the sick, twisted publicity train encircling us right now.

"Caterina, Lucas, over here."

Yeah, they've figured out who I am since yesterday.

"How long you two been dating?"

A wall of photographers and cameramen surrounds us. Most followed us here from her house, but even more were waiting when we arrived. Almost as if they were tipped off. I clench my jaw and stare ahead, continuing to ignore the nonstop questions. It doesn't even faze them.

"Lemme guess…wannabe actor, right? Get in with the daughter so the folks help you out?" I hear the taunt in the man's voice, the desire for me to rise to the bait. I won't… even though he's feeding on the same fears Cat believes to be true. These guys are good.

"Bet it doesn't hurt that she looks like her mom," another one says with a laugh. "Wonder if she acts like her, too?"

That's when I lose it. My head jerks to the side, the words, "Fuck you," spitting out before I can stop myself. Unlike Cat, I'm not wearing sunglasses. I didn't bother with a hat. Nothing hides the anger flashing in my eyes as the camera snaps another shot. The dude in front of me smirks as I realize they won.

"Don't let them get to you," Cat whispers, her lips barely moving. "That's all they want."

She takes my hand and squeezes it. Her understanding makes it worse. Instead of protecting her, my sole purpose for being here today, I served up tomorrow's headline on a silver platter. I knew they were goading me, wanting me to react, and I fell for it. But damn if I could help it.

Life changes in an instant. Yesterday, I had Cat, I had my art, and soccer was soon to be a memory. Sure, my family life was screwed, but isn't everyone's? The important things were coasting along right on track. That is, until her mom pulled that stunt on TV. Then for an encore, she ruined our night at the beach.

Her voice mail said she was flying in today. Apparently, it was *imperative* that they meet as soon as possible. She rattled off information with barely a hello, totally expecting Cat to drop everything to pick her up. And here we are. Never mind that today is a Friday, a *school* day, and that being here meant skipping. Guess things like that don't warrant a blip on Caterina Angeli's radar. It's just further proof that the woman is all about herself…and freaking clueless.

Trying my best to ignore the douche bag inching closer, I squeeze Cat's hand back and say, "I still can't believe your dad went for this." When Cat asked for us to come alone, he agreed as long as we brought an army of security—but even that is lax for him. "Your old man doles out curfews, freaks when your grades slip, and lives for parent-teacher conferences, but lets you ditch school to meet your deranged mother in public." I shake my head and say, "Was he high when you asked?"

Cat gives me a look that I can't read from behind her dark sunglasses, but I'm pretty sure she's rolling her eyes. Her lips definitely twitch. "No, he wasn't high." The word *dork* is all but implied. "Actually, Jenna convinced him."

"Really?" That shocks the hell out of me. I saw the look on her future stepmother's face when we left her house a little while ago. She's as worried about Cat as I am. "*She* thinks this is a good idea?"

Adjusting the purse on her right shoulder, Cat raises to her toes to spy over the crowd. "No, but she said I wasn't a kid anymore. That if this is what I 'think' I need, and it is, she told Dad they should support me." Humor enters her voice as she adds, "She also let it slip that he ditched for Led Zeppelin when he was my age."

Despite the media circus around us, and the knot of anxiety in my gut, I laugh.

She looks back with a grin, and just like that, *my* Cat is back. One hundred percent with me. Air enters my lungs for what feels like the first time today, knowing she's still in there under the façade. Ever since her mom interrupted our beach getaway, Cat's been distracted. Partially with me, but also partially in her head. Thinking about her mom, wondering what this meeting will be like. Planning what she wants to say. Hoping. Some of this she's told me, the rest I just know. Like I know *her*.

She sinks back to her feet as she smiles at the ground. "Thanks for coming with me today."

"Hey." Tugging her closer, I wrap a protective arm around her shoulders and lift her chin with my knuckle so I can look into her eyes. "You couldn't have kept me away if you tried."

Her soft hand encircles my wrist, and she slowly exhales.

My dad doesn't know I'm here, but I can fill a book with the things he doesn't know about me. Mom knows, and she called the school…but if she hadn't, I'd still be here. This is where I belong. As crazy as it sounds, this girl is my home. Where she goes, I follow.

Unfortunately, our stolen moment doesn't last. A sudden buzz of clicks and screams in the distance sets off a fury of commotion around us. At the first scream of "*Caterina,*" Cat's breathing hitches in her throat.

"Where you think you're going?" I ask when she tries to pull away. I tighten my grip on her shoulder, half-teasing, half-serious. My eyes scout the nearest exits as I push my hearing out, listening for how close her mother could be. Cat doesn't try to wrangle free, but the guarded, fake version of her returns—manufactured smile, shoulders rolled back. Calm, collected, and emotionless once more.

"Show time," she whispers.

Two seconds later, the madness reaches a crescendo. I live with a girl, so I've seen *TMZ.* I've watched paparazzi chase down celebrities at this very airport, so I know how it usually plays out. *Most* people ignore them. They wear huge sunglasses like Cat and don baggy clothes. Some wear baseball caps, others hold things over their faces. They never answer questions. They don't speak or encourage the camera-toting asshats in any way.

That's *most* people.

Again, Caterina Angeli breaks the mold.

A tight pack of photographers engulfs her, moving with her as she approaches. Even from here, I can tell she's reveling in the chaos. The limelight pours over her, and she soaks it in, smiling and talking nonstop. She stops to sign a few autographs, flirts with the crowd, and I swear to God, rims her lips with her tongue. Cat's posture goes rigid as she waits for her mom to see her. Acknowledge her presence. Do *something*.

"Okay, boys, that's enough for now," Caterina tells the photographers with a sly grin. "My baby's waiting for me."

One of them asks, "Is that what you're calling Milo these days?" and she throws her head back in a laugh.

"Oh, honey, Milo's just a friend, you know that." Giving the man and his expensive camera an exaggerated wink, she clarifies. "No, my baby is my daughter. Caterina's here to pick up her mama. Isn't that sweet?"

Cat flinches in reflex at the use of her full name, and bile rises in my throat. She carves a hole through the men and looks around until she finally notices Cat, and when she does a smile even faker than the one her daughter is wearing appears.

"Darling, there you are!"

Cat's mask cracks, and for a second, I think she's gonna bolt. But she yanks it back on just in time for the cameras to capture their reunion. Without sparing a glance in my direction, Caterina throws her arms out and rips her daughter away, air kissing and patting her back in an elaborate stage hug. "Oh, aren't you breathtaking?"

"Uh, you, too." Cat's voice sounds strained against the backdrop of camera clicks and calls to *look here*. Her arms remain glued to her sides, her spine ramrod straight. She reaches back, and I quickly grab her hand, letting her tug me forward. Her grip is almost painful as she says, "There's someone I'd like you to meet."

That gets her mom's attention.

Caterina leans back and swings her gaze toward me for the first time. A cougar-like smile stretches her lips. I clench my jaw to keep from saying, "In your dreams, lady." I wouldn't touch this woman with a ten-foot pole. Even if I *weren't* dating her daughter.

"Well, aren't you handsome?" She looks me up and down like I'm a steak dinner, and I throw up a little in my mouth. Darting a glance at Cat, she asks, "And who might this hottie be?"

"This hottie is my *boyfriend*." Her voice is sharp, almost territorial, and it amuses and turns me on at the same time. Believe me, she's got nothing to worry about. Leaning heavily into my side, she says, "Lucas, meet my mom."

It's ironic that she's making introductions. She barely knows the woman herself. But I go with it, thrusting out my hand for a handshake, ignoring her mom's open arms. Like that's happening. This woman really does live in her own world.

With a smirk, Caterina takes my hand and glances back at the cameras. "My daughter's got taste, doesn't she?"

Cat makes a noise in her throat, like a snarling hiss, and I bite my tongue to keep from laughing. We've officially entered Bizarro World.

"I actually have someone I'd like you to meet, too," Caterina continues, her voice rising as her gaze swings back to Cat. "A surprise."

Immediately, I yank my hand back and pull Cat flush against me, wrapping her in the shelter of my arm. Cat hates surprises, and any surprise from this chick can't be good.

Caterina chuckles at my reaction. With a look over her

shoulder, she calls out, "Ransom?"

As I try to figure out whether she's screaming about a kidnapping or calling out a name, a young guy walks up. He has a guitar strapped around his back, and sunglasses hide his eyes. Another boy toy.

This is Cat's so-called surprise? Couldn't she have saved us all time and just sent a grainy picture of them making out on a secluded island? I'm sure there's one floating around somewhere.

But as the guy gets closer, I realize he's young. Like, real young. Maybe just a few years older than me. That cougar smile begins making a whole lot more sense.

"I have an announcement," Caterina says, speaking loudly for the gathered crowd. It's not just paparazzi and security anymore. Travelers have abandoned their awaiting luggage and sappy relatives to gawk at the family reunion happening in Terminal 3. She pulls the young man close to her side while simultaneously reaching for Cat. Thrusting their joined hands in the air, she proudly exclaims, "Meet my family!"

Cat's eyebrows shoot above the rim of her sunglasses. The entire baggage claim area falls silent in curiosity, shock….and the hope for a killer story.

"You already know my beautiful daughter," she says, winking as she kisses the back of Cat's hand. Bright red lipstick stains the skin when she's done. "And now I'd like to introduce you to another special someone. A person who's recently reentered my life, after nineteen long years apart. My *son*, Ransom Chase."

Son?

"Son?" Cat shakes her head, clearly as confused as I am.

The guy is older, which means he was alive when she was born. When she was growing up. Before her mother left.

How could she not know?

The photographers seem to think the same thing, the words *love child* and *affair* whispered not too subtly around us. Cat stumbles back a step before I catch her, her chest rising and falling rapidly. As for Caterina, she just looks *proud,* her trademark wide smile blinding her audience.

"Son," Ransom confirms, yanking his hand back. He walks past his mother, blocking her shot with the cameras, and covers the distance between him and Cat in two quick strides. He pauses to lift his chin at me in acknowledgment, and then looks at his sister. *Sister.* That's still boggling my brain as he says, "It's good to finally meet you."

Cat mumbles a hello. I think she's in shock. Or pissed. I certainly would be if I suddenly discovered I had a sibling I never knew about. In front of the entire world, no less. But then the guy lifts his dark sunglasses on top of his head, and Cat's loud gasp breaks across the terminal.

Cameras click as she jerks back. "*Cipriano*?"

Déjà Vu

·*Cat*·

My proper, reserved Renaissance cousin is decked out in jeans, Chucks, and a fitted Henley. A faux barbed wire strap is slung around his chest, attached to a modern guitar (a style not yet invented in his time), and the only thing I can think is, *it's finally happened*. Blinking repeatedly doesn't change a thing. Cip remains standing there, my mom right beside him, with the paparazzi closing in. I nod with a laugh that I belatedly realize sounds a little manic.

I've officially lost my mind.

Cipriano pokes his tongue in the pocket of his cheek, staring at me in a way that clearly says he agrees, and that's what snaps me out of it.

"What are you... How are you...?" I shake my head and wet my lips, then lift my hands at the craziness of it all. "Did

Reyna send you?"

With an indecipherable glance at Caterina, he says, "I don't think I've met Reyna yet."

I squint, confused, wondering how he got here if not for my favorite gypsy girl—and then his voice registers. His deep, melodic, with a hint of southern twang *modern* voice, and my confusion doubles by a thousand. Why is he talking like that? And how did he learn contractions so quickly? Alessandra *still* struggles with sounding stilted, and she's been here six weeks!

Lucas nudges my arm, subtly clueing me in that I'm gawking like a crazy person. I look around, grateful for the lenses shielding my dazed squint, and quickly pull myself together. At least on the outside. Inside, possibilities are bursting in my mind like mini-explosions. My first thought is that Cipriano is "pulling a Cat," *pretending* to be someone else, just like I did during my trip to the sixteenth century…

Only, the more I stare at this guy, the less likely that theory becomes.

First, the dude in front of me is way too comfortable in his skin. Too *confident*. Sure, Cipriano Angeli was, too, but more in the cool, aloof, boy-next-door, Renaissance hottie sort of way. The brooding musician vibe this guy is rocking takes it to a whole different level. Which leads me to my second point—the guitar pick in his hand. It's not clutched awkwardly, like some random, futuristic prop, the way Alessandra held pens or well, just about anything when she first arrived. This guy's holding his pick like it's an extension of him. Familiar. Reassuring. Which can only mean…

Another freaking doppelganger.

"And the name's Ransom," my cousin's body double

says, emphasizing his name. Correcting me for my public slipup. He holds out a large, calloused hand and adds, "But my friends call me Rance."

Still shocked out of my Louboutins, I do the only thing I can do. I take his hand in mine and watch as a grin curls my alleged brother's lips. Or my alleged *half* brother's lips, since there's no way on earth we share a dad. Dad loves me to death, of that I have no doubt, but I've suffered through enough pitch and catch sessions and football games to know he's always wanted a son, too. If Ransom were his, Dad would've been all over it.

But there's also no denying we're related. Not with that smile. It might not be huge and open like Cipriano's when he first introduced me to his best friend, or even soft and lighthearted like it was during our day in the countryside. Ransom's grin is a simple lip twitch. But the light in his eyes, the slightly crooked mouth, the way it totally transforms his face… It's an undeniable echo of my cousin.

Hayley is going to go utterly gaga over this guy.

And Less will flip her pancake.

"I know who you are," Rance says, taking back his hand and shoving it in the pocket of his low-slung jeans. "When I found out I had a sister, I Googled you."

Great. Considering the highlight reel that's out there, courtesy of the paparazzi, who knows what he unearthed. Or what opinion he's formed of me. The tabloids make up their own truth about who I am, who my family is, and the pictures that sell best are always the most embarrassing. A particularly unflattering shot of me—busting my ass sprawled-eagle-style during a recent family jaunt to the skating rink—springs to mind, and I wince in mortification.

Lucas, ever my protector, and unfortunately, not a party to the inner workings of my mind, stiffens beside me. "Yeah, well, Cat didn't get a heads up about *you* at all."

One scandalicious tidbit, courtesy of dear old mom, is enough for this outing.

"Ransom, this is my boyfriend, Lucas. You have to excuse us if we're overly sensitive, things are just happening kinda fast." I squeeze Lucas's clenched hands and add, "He's just looking out for me."

Behind me, Lucas's chest expands with a breath, and he presses a kiss against my hair.

"Don't sweat it." Rance shoulders his duffle bag and rocks back on his heels. "This isn't easy for any of us." His lips pull down after he says it, and almost as if we're sharing a brain, we both turn to Caterina, watching as she flashes another smile at the cameras.

Then again…

"Maybe we should take this reunion somewhere more private," I suggest. When the woman who gave me birth fails to respond, I raise my voice an octave and say, "*Mom*?"

The title gets her attention.

Swinging that mega smile in our direction, she says, "Of course. A nice, quiet family lunch would be best."

I squint, realizing she had been listening all along, and ponder that nugget as she surveys the crowd.

With a snap of her fingers at a tall man with shaggy blond hair standing a few feet away, she calls, *"Bags!"*

Beckoned, her appointed minion hops to, rolling over a silver cart filled to the brim with luggage. Caterina ducks down, checking to ensure he got everything, and I can't help thinking, *This is probably her packing light.*

Ransom shakes his head with a notable look of disgust and then catches my eye. After holding my gaze for a moment, he grins at me again.

I don't know if it's because he looks so much like my cousin, whom I miss like crazy, or if that mythical sibling bond is an actual thing—but I return it. The needy, abandoned little girl inside me wants to be angry that he's here. That he's stealing my thunder. But I'm not. I'm not even mad at Caterina. This whole day feels like it's happening to someone else, a crazy drama on the CW that no one would ever believe could be true. My life is one big teenage soap opera, and Ransom Chase is the new ratings-boosting plot twist.

At least the casting department got it right.

"All right then." Apparently satisfied, Caterina steps away from the cart with a nod, yanking me back to reality. She flings her long chestnut hair over her shoulder and says, "Who's hungry?"

· · ·

Nice, quiet, family lunch. Those words mock me as we sit at the world-famous restaurant, The Ivy. Honestly, the place itself *is* quaint. A cute cottage with white picket fences and friendly umbrellas on the outside and homey knickknacks on the inside. That's where we are, away from that legendary patio surrounded by cameras. But I know the paparazzi are lurking. Circling the place like hungry sharks. Waiting for a time to attack.

Thanks to Caterina's latest scandal bomb at the airport, the crowd that's been following us has doubled. Also, her phone hasn't stopped ringing, which has made our *nice, quiet reunion* more like an awkward, disjointed, three-ring circus.

In between answering calls from reporters, publicists, and agents, she does at least give us the 411 on how Rance came to be…and why I never knew it. During my mother's first bit role, it would appear she fell in love with a handsome, up and coming costar—a pattern she actually continues to this day, only this time, she ended up preggo. Of course, Caterina didn't realize it until a month later, after the romance had fizzled and filming had wrapped. Young and alone in L.A., her celebrity star rising, Caterina decided it would be best for *Rance* if she quietly placed him up for adoption.

A look about the table confirms we all agree who it was best for. *Her.* But even knowing that, it's hard to argue with the results. Had wolves ended up adopting and raising my half brother, he still would've been better off. At least he was spared the melodrama that's been my life the last sixteen years.

Three years after all of that went down, Mom met Dad, upgrading to sleeping with the assistant director. Thus began my glorious entry into the world. This time Caterina actually told the father, even chose to stick around for a little while… but I think we all knew that had more to do with Dad, his career, and the roles he helped her get than it had to do with me. She doesn't say as much, but it's not hard to read between the lines.

The thing that confuses me is the adoption itself. It was open. Other than claiming she'd checked up on him a few times, Caterina didn't go out of her way to be maternal and she never reached out. But she left the option open for *him* to do so. Why? It makes my mind whirl. Every time I think I get a read on my mother, she does something out of character. Unexpected. She sells me out on television, brings a media circus to the airport—but she came. She's here. She gave up my brother with hardly a backward glance—but she didn't shut him out completely. Wouldn't that have been easier?

Who *is* Caterina Angeli exactly?

"Now that we're all together again," Caterina says, snapping me back to attention, "I'd really like for us to become a family." She tips a glass of wine to her full lips and then plays with the tapered stem as she swallows. If I didn't know better, I'd say she looks nervous. "I know I haven't been the best mother in the world, to either of you, but I want to change that. Maybe the three of us can—" Her cell phone blows up again, cutting off her pretty speech. She glances at the display, looks torn for a moment, then raises a finger and says, "Hold that thought."

Lucas grunts under his breath as she answers the call. He's been silent the whole time, other than giving the waiter his order. I squeeze his hand, silently thanking him again for being here with me, and turn to my new brother. Like Lucas, he hasn't spoken much since we sat down, other than a few monosyllabic responses. Apparently, he reached his word limit at the airport. "So…music, huh?"

His green and black speckled guitar pick continues its seamless, fluid transition from one knuckle to the next. "Yep."

O-kay. Not much to go on, and still one syllable. But hey, it's something.

Don't ask me why I care or why I feel the need to drag him into a conversation. I don't know why. I just do. Life dealt me a crappy pair of cards for sure, but at least I had

Dad.

Did Rance have *anyone*?

That thought has me scooting my chair forward. "What kind do you play?" I'd rather ask about his adoptive family—are they nice, does he have a good home, any siblings—but figure it's best to start small.

He shrugs. "Eclectic. I like grunge, alternative…nineties rock, like Sublime and Pearl Jam. I also dig the classics. Jeff Beck, Jerry Garcia…" He trails off with a shrug, like those names are self-explanatory.

"Awesome," I enthuse, even though I don't have a clue. Those names mean nothing to me. I'm 99 percent sure Ben and Jerry's has an ice cream flavor named after the last dude, but that's apparently the extent of my *eclectic* music knowledge.

My boyfriend, on the other hand, suddenly leans his elbows on the table. "Nice taste," he says. I look over to see his lips pressed together as though he's suddenly interested in our conversation. "Do you have a band at home?" he asks. "An agent?"

"No agent." As he says this, the waiter places the check at our table and Caterina, still on the phone, rolls her eyes and points to the shaggy blond at the table behind us. "I have a few guys I gig with, but nothing too structured."

Ransom leans back to pocket his guitar pick, and I elbow Lucas in the ribs. "I know what you're doing," I whisper.

Sliding his arm behind my chair, he whispers back, "Just looking out for my girl."

The warmth in his eyes makes my heart melt, even as I heave a sigh. Doesn't he grasp that we're already on this runaway train? All we can do now is hold on and see where the crazy takes us. I'm not saying that discovering I have a brother isn't freaky as all get out. It *is*. But it's not like it's Rance's fault. If anything, he has more of a reason to be angry with me. I've known who my mother is my entire life. Yeah, she ditched me with a quickness, but she left him at *birth*.

And to be honest, as life changing as it is having Ransom here, he does alleviate some of the pressure. I'm still determined to get answers, but Caterina Angeli in the flesh is a lot to take. For now, I'm totally cool with baby steps.

"And where's home?" I ask, not ready to give up yet.

"Houston," he answers.

That explains the twang.

"Do you have a girlfriend there?"

Lucas lifts an eyebrow, and I pull a face, elbowing him again. He's only teasing, but seriously, ew. I'm not crushing on my half brother. This isn't Jerry Springer. I'm just trying to get to know Ransom better...and maybe doing a little fact-finding for Hayley.

"Nope."

Before I can ask anything else, Caterina ends her call. Rance stretches his arms over his head, sneaks a peek at our mother's minion, and then cranes his neck toward the entrance. "So what's the plan to get out of here?"

Sliding her phone into her purse, Mom wrinkles her smooth brow in confusion. "What do you mean?"

The three of us look at her like she's deranged. She can't be serious. But when she continues staring back with complete curiosity, I realize she is. *Oh, good Lord.*

A migraine begins mounting behind my eye sockets. "The paparazzi have to be even worse by now," I explain.

"Isn't this their home away from home?"

Which is why this is the last place on earth I'd ever come if given the choice. Don't get me wrong, the food's great. But crowds, attention, expectations…that's my trifecta of nightmares. My goal in life is to blend. Hard to do when your parents are famous, but with Dad's weirdo rules and cling to normalcy, it hasn't been impossible. Blending with Caterina Angeli around, however, is a joke.

Mom waves her hand in the air. "Most of them are harmless if you give them what they want. The world is just excited to get to know my kids; that's all. We'll simply go out there, smile, and let them take their pictures while the valet brings the car around." She shrugs her dainty shoulders. "It'll be fine."

She nods at the blond dude, a signal of some sort, and he taps his knuckle on our table en route to the hostess stand. I desperately hope he's asking to have our car brought around. Caterina pushes to her feet, tucks her chair back under the table, and then looks at the three of us expectantly. Evidently, this portion of the day is over.

"Well, this was a lovely first lunch," she says as we grab our things. Another one of Caterina's minions whisked most of their luggage to the hotel earlier, but Rance had refused to part with his guitar. As he slings the strap around his chest, our mother says, "I hope you don't mind, but I've requested a cab to take Ransom and me back to the hotel. It's been an eventful day, and I need to lie down."

"Oh," I say, making a face. When did she request that? Whenever she wasn't on the phone, she was talking with us, filling us in on our sordid past.

Had this been the plan all along? To eat and ditch? So

much for reconnecting.

Honestly, though, today *has* been a day of revelations. And a roller coaster of emotions. Second-guessing myself, trying to get a handle on my mother, probing for info with my brother. I've had just about all that I can take. Getting space to decompress sounds great…but knowing *she* wants the same stings like crazy.

I pull on my familiar plastic smile, not wanting to let on that I'm upset. That would show weakness, something I swore I'd never do around her. "Of course," I say. "When will I see you again?"

Crap, did that sound too eager?

My mother smiles as she slides her mega purse on her shoulder. "I'll see you tomorrow, darling." She chuckles like I'm being daft, and I wrinkle my eyebrows. "At the wedding, remember?"

Oh yeah. *That.*

In light of the world discovering the details, and then parking themselves on our front lawn, it's no big secret that Dad's wedding is in limbo. Right along with Jenna's diet. When I caught her scarfing a thick slab of fudge last night, she just shrugged. "Times like these demand chocolate," she said.

There's no arguing with that logic.

"Actually," I say, "Dad and Jenna postponed it."

Caterina's smile fractures as color leeches from her face. I watch, wide-eyed, as she reels back and then grasps her chair for support. "*What*?"

Silence.

The quiet din of conversation, the *clank* of utensils around us, ceases.

We're the center of attention. Again.

Patrons of The Ivy are used to hobnobbing celebrities. Bigwigs come here all the time; it's part of the restaurant's charm. But familiarity didn't stop the subtle stares and whispers those patrons had been casting in our direction for the last hour. Caterina Angeli *is* on a different level, I guess. Especially with the gossip bombs she's dropped during the last twenty-four hours. The Kardashian family has nothing on her. But now that she's made a spectacle, she's declared open season.

Cell phones whip out, pictures snap, and excited murmurs rise. All while Caterina's eyes flash with emotion. *What* emotion I couldn't say, because sadly my own mother is a stranger, one even more confusing than yesterday. But the woman who exudes assurance and works the cameras like a supermodel is gone.

I turn to exchange gobsmacked looks with my boyfriend and new brother. Of course, they're dudes, so they're zero help, but it's not as if this is exactly *my* territory, either. I don't do emotions well. Before Jenna and Alessandra, I didn't do them at all. This girly stuff is still new for me. Am I supposed to offer her a hug or defend my dad's decision?

Reyna really should've given me an instruction manual.

Thankfully, Caterina pulls herself together on her own. The Hollywood smile returns as she glances about the room and asks in a gentler voice, "When did that happen?" Followed quickly with, "And why?"

She wants to know *why*? Either my mother is fishing for intel or she really is as self-involved as I'd always imagined. She was married to my dad; shouldn't she know how private he is?

True anger, for the first time since catching her on *The Kate Lyons Show*, boils under my skin. You can mess with me all you want, but I'm a daddy's girl. He's the one person I've always been able to count on. Indignation on his behalf churns in my gut, and before I can check it, I spit out, "Last night. After the details were leaked on national television and Dad came home to forty-seven bloodsuckers harassing his family for a quick buck."

My mother winces at my sharp tone. Lucas snorts. And Ransom snaps his fingers.

"Time to jet," my half brother says, and before I can wonder if my response came out too harsh, I'm yanked from the table. Rance nods as Lucas steers me toward the exit, toward the chaos we only recently escaped. And away from my shell-shocked mother and patrons who are no doubt tweeting as we speak.

I slide on my sunglasses seconds before we step outside. Even with the dark lenses, I feel exposed when I see how large the crowd has grown. With my yummy lobster ravioli considering a comeback, I look to Lucas, who points beyond the cameras to his shiny black car idling near the curb. Thank God.

"Ready?" he asks.

I nod, unable to speak, and we run for it, dashing through the packed patio and out through the white picket fence. On principle, I *never* dash. That, along with emotions, is a sign of weakness, and I prefer acting as though the cameras and attention don't bother me. But at this point, no one's buying that anyway. Even if they did, I no longer care. I just want *out.*

Jack is waiting dutifully at the sidewalk, and with the

help of his team, they push the paparazzi aside. Lucas throws open the passenger door, and I scoot my butt in, locking eyes with Ransom just before the door closes. With the yells, questions, and general nuttiness around him, he looks lost. Lonely. And a bit curious.

Strange that I can read him so well, when I can't do the same with my own mother.

I lift my hand in a wave as Lucas jumps in on his side. Most of the cameras are tracking Caterina, so they flock to the cab behind us, giving us an easy exit. As Lucas peels away from the curb, I turn in my seat, and watch as Rance raises his hand in good-bye.

Seeing Double

·Lucas·

My foot is glued to the accelerator. Somewhere behind me, Jack is probably cursing me out, but I don't care. My only goal right now is to get Cat away from the drama. Away from the insanity following us and from her crazy-ass mother.

Gritting my teeth, I check my mirrors and change lanes. Cat's phone beeps from the center console, the first sound to break the silence since we tore away from The Ivy. She glances down to read the text.

"Mom wants to have lunch again tomorrow," she says with a sigh. "With everyone this time. Guessing by everyone she means Dad and Jenna."

Of course she does. Whatever else this may be about, it also involves being seen together often.

When we come to a four-way stop, I turn to her and ask,

"What do you want to do?"

I know what *I* want to do. Tell the woman to get lost. But this isn't my call. I meant it when I said that I'd stand by her no matter what. Doesn't mean I have to like it, though.

With a sigh, she begins typing a response. "They need to all sit down eventually, but this time it's gonna be on my turf." Each click of the keys is magnified in the quiet car. When she's done, she sighs and drops her phone in her purse. "This is so crazy."

I glance in my rearview mirror and then back at her. "What's crazy?"

Cat turns in her seat, sliding a leg under her, and drags her teeth over her bottom lip. It doesn't hide the vulnerable smile lifting her perfect mouth. "I have a brother." Her voice is soft and almost dreamlike, and damn if that doesn't get to me.

The tough girl who keeps everyone at a distance is disappearing. Her prodigal mother returns, some random dude in tow, and Cat's usual go-to defenses get jacked. It makes me want to bang my head against the dash.

Caterina spent the entire lunch practically ignoring the children she abandoned and then brought together in a media firestorm. Her *public* was more important. As for Cat's newfound brother, I just don't trust him.

Ransom Chase is Caterina's son. Besides the obvious physical similarities, her team of lawyers and agents had to have vetted the guy out. But what I want to know is why did he come forward *now*? What does this guy want? Has it escaped everyone's attention that he's a musician, a career that would benefit from celebrity connections?

Stealing another glance at Cat, I release a breath and

turn at the light. I'm glad she's opening her heart and trusting more. She should. Most days, she's surrounded by people who care and want to protect her.

Caterina Angeli and this mysterious son of hers? They are *not* those people.

"Luc, I can't tell you how many times I wished for that growing up," Cat says, idly playing with the A/C vent. "A big brother to tell off the mean girls who teased me about Mom or beat up the guys who expected me to be like her. And, God, the fact that he's a doppelganger..." She trails off with a shake of her head as if she's processing a million thoughts.

My focus is on one.

Another doppelganger. Meaning in addition to the others, including *me*. A fun revelation from the night I discovered Alessandra was a time traveler. Apparently, look-alikes aren't just a dumb plot device on chick television; they actually exist. I've seen the proof. Snapshots from Cat's stay in the sixteenth century of Alessandra's mother, who looks just like Caterina, and the guy who looks exactly like me. Lorenzo.

Cat's first boyfriend.

So what if it was only a nine-day relationship. It might not have anything on six weeks, but Lorenzo Cappelli owns her first kiss. He's the reason—well, he and her Renaissance ancestors—that Cat started letting people in to begin with. Lorenzo is also the reason she fought our connection so hard in the beginning. She was still hung up on *him*.

"He's a part of my past, Luc. But you hold my future."

That's what Cat told me the night I found out about him. As Alessandra broke the news to Austin that she'd soon be returning to her own time, or so we thought, Cat dragged me away to talk. I was still reeling from seeing Lorenzo's picture and the portrait he'd painted of her, but I remember thinking that I was being an ass. Austin was telling his girl good-bye forever, and I was pissed that mine once had feelings for some other guy.

But that's just it. Lorenzo wasn't just *some* other guy. He was a guy who looked exactly like me. After a month of her pushing me away, we'd finally gotten together, and all I could wonder was if Cat really wanted *me* or if I was simply a fill-in-the-blank understudy.

Old insecurities crept back in. Whispers that I'll never be enough—for Cat or for Dad. That the best I'll ever be is second place, a stand in for David and Lorenzo. But Alessandra fighting fate was bigger than my doubts, so I brushed them off. Told her it was no big deal, and since then, I've acted like it doesn't bother me at all. Hell, I've got the girl.

But every once in a while I can't help wondering, do I really?

That thought continues to prick at me as we pull up to her house. Her dad's Altima and Jenna's Lexus sit in the driveway, and only a few hard-core stalkerazzi are camped outside the gate. The rest are probably in front of her mom's hotel. As I shove my hands in my pockets and slog my way to the door, I glance at the two photographers closest to me.

The first is young, maybe ten years older than I am, and has a manic gleam in his eyes. He snaps pics like he's hyped up on speed. He's either hungry for a story or desperate— probably both.

The other man, though, is who grabs my attention. Dark hair shot with gray, he looks tired. It's just after three in the afternoon, but I feel his pain. When he lifts his camera, he takes his time, calmly composing each photo before pushing the shutter button. Right now, that careful, observant eye is focused on me, standing stock-still on the driveway.

"Lucas?"

Cat is already at the front door, probably wondering what's wrong with me. Hell if I know, but I don't move. The older man raises his eyes from his lens and looks at me. Just looks at me. Then he lifts his camera again, and without knowing why, I lift my fingers in a wave. I wait for the telltale click and then follow my girl inside.

. . .

Cat taps her nails on the dark cherry tabletop. Other than that, the dining room is dead silent. She just gave her dad and Jenna the rundown of the day's events—the chaos at the airport and the even worse lunch. As she did, a bit of the old Cat came back, appearing more curious than eager about Ransom and generally distrustful of her mom. The thing is, though, because of who her parents are, Cat is an expert chameleon. She can read a room in an instant and subtly transform herself into the girl she thinks people expect. It's so second nature that I'm not sure she even realizes when she's doing it. But I do.

Her dad does, too. I can tell from the way he's watching her that he's not quite buying it, either. He'd already known some of the details before we arrived—Jenna spent the morning glued to every entertainment site in existence, knowing today's reunion would be headline news. As a result, they actually witnessed the whole *surprise you've got a brother* portion live.

Mr. Crawford looks like he could use a stiff drink. I can't help but feel for him. At one point, he loved the woman. After all, he married her, and unlike a lot of Hollywood players, that actually means something to him. Finding out your ex-wife had another kid and never bothered to tell you about it can't be easy.

As the silence stretches, Jenna and I exchange bewildered glances. I sure as hell don't know what to do or say here. Jenna scrunches her mouth and then opens it, just as I hear the front door open.

"Hello?"

Alessandra's accented voice carries down the hall, and Jenna replies, "In here!"

Her eyes meet mine, and I can tell she's thinking the same thing I am. *Rescued.*

Cat's cousin always knows what to say. As good as I am at reading Cat, Alessandra is better. Glancing at Mr. Crawford, I wonder if he ever finds it strange that his loner daughter bonded so quickly with a foreign exchange student. That's the cover story they're selling to explain Alessandra's presence. But I guess in the end, he's her dad, and he's just happy to see her finally engaging. Besides, it's not as if he'd ever believe the truth.

A minute later, Alessandra enters the room, her sweet smile in place, followed by Austin and his smirk.

"Look, Velma, the Scooby gang back together again."

Across the table, Jenna's concerned look fades. So does Mr. Crawford's distant one. Cat relaxes in her high-backed chair, and I send Austin a subtle nod.

I've known the guy for a month—hell, I've only lived

in the States again for three—but I know him pretty well. He's not that complex. If it doesn't involve Alessandra, his sister Jamie, or surfing, Austin doesn't give a shit. But I like that about him. It's refreshing to hang out with someone who doesn't have a hidden agenda. The crowd I ran with back in Milan, that's all they had. Being so straightforward also makes Austin easy to read. From his calculated, playful expression, and Alessandra's nervous twitches, it's obvious they know what went down today, and that's why he's here.

Austin came to do what Austin does best. *Deflect.*

Hitching his hip onto the polished table, Austin *tsks* under his breath. "Princess, correct me if I'm wrong, but didn't Cat give me grief recently about finding my way to class?"

Alessandra chuckles under her breath before replying, "Yes, I believe she did."

Austin nods, then shakes his head, *tsking* again. "Thought so. But see, even on my worst day, back before you taught me the error of my ways, I could at least find the *building.*"

As if their gypsy chanted her hocus-pocus, the tension from the room dissipates.

The dude is good.

"Yeah, yeah," Cat says, rolling her eyes. "You caught us. Lucas and I ditched, but at least we had parental permission. *And* a good reason."

Austin slaps his chest with mock offense. "Are you implying surfing isn't a good reason?"

"Yep." Cat smiles playfully, then slides a look at her dad. "Neither is Led Zeppelin."

This time it's Mr. Crawford who rolls his eyes. Like father, like daughter. Leaning over to ruffle Cat's hair, he says, "I've failed in my parenting if you believe that's true."

We all laugh, and the room seems to take a collective breath. Comic relief. I guess if we're the Scooby gang, that would make Austin our Shaggy.

"Well, I think I saw another box of brownie mix in the pantry," Jenna says, sliding her chair back against the hardwood floor. "I'll go whip up some snacks."

"And I'll go watch ESPN," Cat's dad says, also pushing out of his seat. "That should be a relatively safe channel. They don't give a rat's ass about Hollywood."

His mouth tips in a teasing smile, but his eyes are tight. Patting Cat on the shoulder, he walks past us to head for the living room, and Cat offers, "The Game Show Network is another good option!"

After he's disappeared around the corner, she sighs and looks back at the three of us. "My life is stranger than fiction."

"Certainly never a dull moment," Alessandra agrees with a strained smile. Then she tilts her head. "That is the expression, right?"

Cat smiles. "You got it." Blowing out a breath, she pushes to her feet and links her hand in mine. Just that small connection makes me feel calm. With a gentle tug, she pulls me toward her, saying, "Follow me, everyone."

One by one, we file down the hall and into Cat's bedroom. It's a scene eerily similar to a night not that long ago. The night I found out the truth about Alessandra…and about Lorenzo.

Fighting to keep my eyes straight ahead, away from the painting on her wall, I head for her bed. Cat has no idea the portrait bothers me. If she did, she'd take it down. But who wants to be the jealous dude who can't get over his girl's ex? Not me. I'm *not* that guy—not normally. I've had plenty of girlfriends before, and none of their pasts ever bothered me.

This is just the first ex-boyfriend I've been related to. Or who could be my twin.

And the girl is *Cat.*

Falling onto the mattress, Cat bounces slightly and then yanks me down beside her. I twist to put my back against the headboard and tug her flush against me. Having her in my arms helps. Cat takes a deep breath and sinks into my chest, waving her hand at the big, open bed.

"Sit. Stay. Join us. There is news to be shared."

"That sounds ominous." Austin plops on the other end and glances around, and I have a feeling he's remembering that other night, too.

Alessandra moves to sit next to him, but before she can, Cat lifts her palm. "Actually, Less, do you mind grabbing my *binder* first?"

Less's eyebrows shoot up at the emphasized word. By now, we all know what that means. The hidden binder filled with proof of time travel impossibilities. Wordlessly, Alessandra turns to Cat's desk and rifles under the false bottom in the third drawer. When she emerges a moment later with a bright purple binder, my breath freezes in my lungs. So much for not being the jealous douche.

"Why do we need this?" Alessandra asks, tapping the plastic-coated cover. I can imagine the fight she's having with herself, wanting to flip the pages, see her parents and hometown again, and being scared of the result. She's acclimating to our world amazingly well, and to look at her, you'd never think she has a down moment. But I know this isn't easy. Cat's told me that she struggles with homesickness. She probably always will.

"Trust me, girl, I wouldn't be pulling this out on you unless I thought it was important." Cat carefully takes the binder from her hand, clasping her fingers for a long moment before letting them go. "But there's something that Lucas and Austin need to see to understand."

I watch, confused, as she turns page after page, quickly scanning each picture. Austin's holding Alessandra in his arms, and even from across the bed, I can see her hands trembling. Glancing at the book, images bleed and meld as they fly past, almost unrecognizable—except for the one of Lorenzo. When I catch that one, I immediately wish I could see Cat's face, see if she reacted at all. Her body language didn't change. Her fingers didn't twitch. Her torso didn't flinch. But I can't help but wonder. I hate the insecure guy I become thinking of him.

Luckily, that's forgotten a couple pages later when Cat stops on a picture of Ransom. Only, it's not Ransom. It's a guy who looks exactly like him, except dressed in a weird jacket and tights. Unfortunately, the picture she has of Lorenzo is only a face shot. Seeing him dressed like *this* would help the ego a lot.

"Is that Cipriano?" I ask, remembering the name she said at the airport.

Cat nods, and Alessandra makes a sound like a choked sob. I take it she and this guy were close. This is going to be tricky.

"Less, you know I'd never hurt you on purpose, but I thought the guys should see this before my new brother comes over. I also wanted to prepare *you*…"

The slight confusion that washes over their faces says they knew *about* Rance; they just have no clue what he looks like. They must've been in class, where we should've been, and away from social media when Caterina introduced him to the world.

"Sweetie, Ransom is the twenty-first-century Cip."

As Alessandra gingerly accepts the binder from Cat, I take out my phone. With a quick tap of my fingers, I pull up thousands of photos from today's airport soiree. Sure enough, the one of me spitting fire after the crude remark about Cat is popular. I find one of Ransom without sunglasses and catch Austin's attention, waving my phone in the air before handing it to him.

Austin's eyes grow wide as he looks at the phone, then at the binder, then at the phone again. "Baby." He nudges her gently, and Alessandra lifts her head up from the picture. He hands over the phone and wraps her tighter in his arms as she gasps.

"That was my reaction," Cat says, slumping against me. "If you think about it, though, it makes sense. My mom is your mom's doppelganger. It's not that crazy that their sons would be each other's." Ah, so Cipriano must be Alessandra's brother. Shit, that sucks. "I wonder if Rance's dad looks like Uncle Marco," she muses.

No one answers. The four of us just sit there, Alessandra mourning the loss of her family, Austin consoling her, and me just enjoying the feel of having Cat in my arms away from the madness. When a knock sounds on the door several minutes later, she bolts up, Less scrambles, and I slam the binder shut just as Jenna walks in.

"Your father and I would rather this door stay open,"

she says, carrying a tray of brownies in her hand. Jenna sets the tray on the middle of the bed, between all of us, and glances curiously at the closed binder. "What's that?"

Cat being Cat of course couldn't leave it unmarked. Pencil sketches of Italy, period costumes, and Michelangelo's David cover the entire thing.

The four of us stare at one another, mouths gaping, as Jenna leans forward. "Is this a scrapbook from our trip?" she asks, picking it up.

We all find our voices at the same time. "No!"

Jerking upright, Jenna yelps as the binder drops from her fingertips like a dead weight. Her hand flies to her chest, no doubt in shock from what appears to be an extreme overreaction—extreme and suspicious. Sure enough, her lips press together, and her eyes narrow on each of us.

The chances of her putting it all together if she takes a peek at the book is highly unlikely. She'll be confused, but probably nothing we couldn't explain away...at least until she stumbled across a picture of Alessandra's mom, Lorenzo, or Cipriano. But with everything else going to crap, I'd rather not tempt fate.

"Sorry, Ms. J," I say, smiling to flash the dimples that work wonders on girls my own age. I'm not flirting with Cat's future stepmom. That would be weird. And gross. But I'm not above using every weapon in my arsenal to keep this ship from going up in flames. "It's just a project we're working on for Mr. Scott. A surprise for the midterm art expo."

At least that's not too much of a stretch. Cat and I are working on a project for the expo. It just has jack to do with anything in that binder.

"Hmm." Jenna fists her hand on her hip, looking like she doesn't want to believe me. But after a moment, she relents. "All right. But this door is staying open, okay?"

We all mumble various forms of "no problem" as she backs away, and then listen in silence until the click of her shoes disappears.

Cat falls back against me. "Holy close calls, Batman."

"Tell me about it," I mutter, and then press a kiss against her hair.

Austin snaps his fingers. "Well, before you three bad influences corrupt me any further, I gotta go." He stands, and Alessandra follows him, latching on to his arm. "I have to bring Jamie to her dance class tonight."

She nods, and they do this unspoken communication thing where they stare at each other and smile. It's sweet, but nauseating. Mainly because Cat and I were headed to that place before the world came crashing on our heads.

"Later, man." I raise my fist, and Austin bumps it.

Cat snatches his hand before it drops.

"The wedding's postponed," she says, "but I still need you here for lunch tomorrow. Caterina and Rance are coming for a *family* meal, this time on my turf, and like you said, you're a part of us now." Flicking her gaze to Alessandra, she adds, "Plus, I think my girl here may need the backup."

"I'll be there," he promises, tucking Less under his arm.

As I watch them walk out the door, in that solid zone that I want for Cat and me, I remember another thing about tomorrow. Something I almost forgot in the drama of today, and something much better than a meal with her deranged mother. With that in mind, it looks like I better head out, too.

Sliding her hair to one side, I say, "I should go." I lower

my lips to her exposed shoulder and breathe in the sweet scent of her skin.

Cat leans into my touch, tugging on my arms until they're wrapped around her tiny waist. She folds her arms around them, hugging me close, and lets her head fall back against my chest. Inhaling deeply, she says, "No, you shouldn't."

I chuckle as she relaxes her hold, only to drag her fingernails across the skin of my forearms. The feel of her touch sends fire coursing through my body.

"You should stay here with me," she continues, drawing lazy patterns over my flesh. Tension coils at the base of my spine. The contrast of her light, sun-kissed skin against my darker tones, the gentle rake of her fingernails, makes my stomach knot. I have to taste her.

Placing my hand under Cat's chin, I tilt her head back and brush my lips over hers. But a brush isn't enough. This girl turns me inside out, and I should've known I'd need more. I'll always need more. It's not just a physical thing. The scent of her hair, the feel of her lips, the truth that she's mine…it rushes to my head. I don't care that the door is open. I forget that I need to leave. My hands are in her hair, her hands are clutching my thighs, and the whimper in her throat belongs to me.

When her full lips part and the tiniest flick of her tongue touches mine, any shred of control I had snaps.

Grabbing her hips, I spin her around until she's facing me, only breaking the kiss to position her how I want. Before I take her mouth again, Cat's heated gaze meets mine, and she smiles. Another piece of my heart is hers.

A sound down the hall minutes later breaks through my mental fog. I don't want to stop. My hands are on Cat's face and up the back of her shirt, and she's just so damn soft. But we need to. I have plans to make, and if her dad finds us like this, tomorrow is not going to go the way I want.

Groaning, I drop my head to her shoulder. "I really do have to go," I say again.

Knowing it and doing it are two different things, though. I can't stop touching her. Sliding my hand across the smooth skin of her back, I make a mental list of things to do before tomorrow night, trying to get my blood back up to my head. When I remember my first stop—the living room to talk with Cat's dad—I find that dose of cold water I need.

"But hey," I say, sliding my nose over her rose-scented skin, "do me a favor, okay? No stressing tonight. If you get upset or worried, call me. We can talk all night, or I'll come back over. But try to get some sleep. You've got a big day tomorrow."

I press my lips to her throat because I can't help it. Cat wiggles in my lap, so I force myself to stop. She grumbles. "I know," she says with a sigh. "Lunch with the family."

Grinning, I lift my head. "Nope. Not just lunch. Now that the wedding is postponed, I get you for the rest of the night. And I've got plans. Big plans."

"Plans?" Cat's slightly swollen lips pucker, and all I can think about is tasting them again. But then they lift into a gorgeous smile and form the words, "Valentine's Day."

"Valentine's Day," I confirm, unable to stop myself from leaning in and stealing one more kiss. Her hands fist my shirt, and I smile against her lips. "And, Miss Crawford, you best prepare yourself, because you're gonna swoon your ass off."

Game Face

·*Cat*·

Lunch with the Crawford/Angeli family is about as weird and awkward as you would imagine. Which is to say, *very*. From the moment my mom and brother walked in, Alessandra's been glued to Ransom's side, interchangeably gawking and staring off into the distance. Eventually, I hope having him here will be like a gift from fate (or more accurately, Reyna). A way of bringing Less a taste of home, something familiar. Right now, though, it's just a big ball of weird.

As for Rance, he's too busy texting to notice my cousin's stares, and Austin keeps cracking inappropriate jokes. Lucas is silently watching everyone, and Jenna is uncomfortable, and no doubt a little insecure, so she's all over the place, strung higher than normal, and chattering faster than Michael Phelps cuts through water. As for Dad and

Caterina, they're sitting on opposite ends of the table for a reason. Other than a private conversation right after they arrived, my guess about my brother, they've barely looked at each other. It's safe to say the olive branch he extended via wedding invitation has been snapped in half.

Me? I've got my game face back on.

After Lucas left yesterday, it took a while for me to come down from my kissy stupor. But when I did, I crashed and burned. The culmination of discovering my mother had a secret love child, seeing her be as self-absorbed as I always feared, and the surprising hints of a real woman with depth sent me on an energy spiral. Less and I made an unspoken pact not to discuss any of it, instead choosing to spend the evening vegged out in front of the television. I've totally got her hooked on *Family Feud*.

But after a restless night of sleep, my eyes popped open this morning, and I could've sworn I heard Reyna's voice floating in my room. At the very least, I remembered the lesson she sent me to the past to learn.

I'm a type A girl. I prefer things color-coded, organized, and within my control. Unfortunately, sometimes life sucks, and it rarely goes according to plan. My trip to the sixteenth century taught me that while I can't control other people, or the actions that happen around me, I *can* control how I react. I might not have Caterina figured out yet, but that doesn't matter. This isn't *her* ship to command. It's mine.

And I'm on a mission for normalcy.

"The meal was lovely, Jenna," my mother says, dabbing the corner of her mouth with a beige linen napkin. "Thank you. I hope we weren't any trouble, inviting ourselves over like this on such short notice. I'd hate to think we interrupted any of your plans."

The overly bright smile my future stepmother has worn all morning fractures. Caterina has the good sense to wince. As Lucas squeezes my hand under the table, I catch Dad's Papa Bear frown fall into place.

The elephant in the room is about to throw up.

"Just our wedding," Jenna declares in a tight, controlled voice, her blond hair bouncing with the sharp shake of her head. Austin chokes, then coughs to cover it up as she places her hands on the table and pushes to her feet. "Excuse me, Peter, I have to go check on…" Mouth open, her gaze falls to our half-empty plates and the carved pie resting in the center of the table. Dad squeezes her hand. Unable to come up with a reason to bolt, other than she wants to, Jenna shrugs and simply says, "Excuse me."

Caterina looks shell-shocked. Ransom actually puts down his phone. He glances at me, and even from across the table, I can see the humor shining in his eyes. It's safe to say the strained-yet-civil tone of the last half hour has been obliterated. But I can't help but be proud of Jenna. That was a huge step for the bubbly woman, and I'd bet my brand spanking new paintbrushes she's in the kitchen right now doing a fist pump.

Dad tosses his balled-up napkin onto his plate. "I'll be back."

Mom gnaws on her full bottom lip as he clears the room. "Guess I put my foot in it, huh?"

More like *buried* her foot, but there's no point in correcting her. Especially not when she actually looks apologetic. I'm not an idiot. I know my mother's an actress, so faking emotions is kind of her gig…but honestly, this looks legit.

Unfortunately, I also can't argue with the facts, so I ignore what I hope is a rhetorical question and say, "How long are the two of you staying in town?"

Caterina's attention flicks to Ransom, who shifts in his seat. This is the first time since I've met the dude that he's appeared almost flustered. Uncomfortable. An impressive feat considering the crap we've been dealing with. Our mother's teeth sink farther into her lip before she releases it. "Well, actually, I plan to stay for the next two weeks. I have a few meetings lined up, things to do, and I hoped to spend some time getting to know you. The both of you. In fact, I'd like the pair of you to join me at an event on Thursday."

She gives me what appears to be a genuine, hopeful smile, one that makes her eyes light up, and the shift sends me reeling. She keeps flipping the switch. Narcissistic one minute, humble the next. She reveals family secrets on national television and drops bombs in front of the stalkerazzi, then comes here for a private lunch and seems almost…normal. Not *my* kind of normal. Even at her most laidback, there's no mistaking Caterina's a starlet. But she's nearly relatable.

These hidden layers are seriously messing with my head.

Dad returns a few moments later and takes his seat, announcing to the silent room, "Jenna will be out in just a minute. She's on the phone with a client." That's a rather convenient story if I've ever heard one, but I'll go with it. Dad pops his neck, a clear sign he's feeling the tension of the room, then leans back and glances first at my mother and then at me. His eyes narrow. "What did I miss?"

"I've invited Caterina to join me at an event Thursday,"

my mother replies, again with my full given name, invoking an inward groan.

I detest my name. Partially because it's *her* name and partially because it just sounds pretentious. Ill-fitting. I'm not exotic or glamorous or cool enough to pull off *Caterina*. I'm Cat, pure and simple. But I bite my tongue. We already have enough drama to deal with today.

Lucas links our fingers together, and the gentle reassurance has my shoulders descending from my ears. He's been quiet for the last hour. Just before he came over, his dad's partner from Milan showed up at his door. The man said he had meetings at the LA office, but for some reason, Lucas doesn't seem to buy it. His right leg is bouncing, and he's distracted. The wheels in his brain are clearly churning, turning over this guy's visit again and again like some weird ruminating cow. I don't know why this bothers him so much, and now isn't the time, but I squeeze his hand and make a mental note to ask him about it tonight.

Tonight.

The highlight of this wacky day gone awry. Chill bumps explode down my arms just thinking about our date, wondering where he's taking me. What surprises he has up his sleeve. The boy is a romantic—it's the artist side of him—and he never fails to make me feel special. And turned on.

"What kind of event?" Dad asks, steepling his fingers on the tabletop.

For a second, I think he's asking about our date. Warmth fills my cheeks as I lower my lashes to avoid eye contact. Dad and I may be close, but we draw the line at dishing the deets about our love lives...especially now that I actually have one.

But then Mom answers.

"The premiere for the latest Holly Underhill film," she says. "The director is a friend of mine, and I thought it would be something fun the kids and I could do together."

The way she keeps calling us *the kids* rankles about as much as hearing her spew my full name. I'm not the five-year-old little girl she left behind. I'm sixteen. And Ransom is nineteen, already an adult. But hey, at least she wants to hang out with me. That's an improvement over the last ten years.

The stupid, foreign hope I felt at the beach springs to life again inside me. The one that makes me think it's possible that she really has changed, despite the media circus yesterday. That maybe, just maybe, we can have some semblance of a mother/daughter relationship. If not a normal one, at least one that isn't fractured beyond repair.

Dad taps his lips twice, drags in a deep breath, then squeezes his temples. "Thursday is a school night."

He closes his eyes as if in pain, and I imagine I can see the good and bad angels screaming in his ears. They look a lot like Jenna and Caterina.

The bad angel is reminding Dad that this is what he's always wanted for me—a chance to know my mother. To figure out the other half of my DNA, get over my trust issues, and officially move on from the past. Since things got serious with Jenna, he's been urging me to embrace our new family unit. In many ways, I have. Jenna's and my relationship is leaps and bounds better than it was a few months ago, thanks to my trip to the past. Spending a week in the sixteenth century gave me a fresh perspective on my present. My aunt helped me appreciate Jenna's wonderful traits and realize that there was room in Dad's life for both of us, even though my future stepmom and I are so drastically different. But it wasn't a miracle cure.

Meanwhile, the good angel is recapping how hard he's worked to shelter me from the business. Dad's über-protective, so while I do go with him to events from time to time, say a film location or to one of his premieres, I'm usually whisked into the theater on arrival as he gives his requisite sound bite. Something tells me Caterina will have her newly reunited family standing right beside her on the red carpet.

"Do you *want* to go to a premiere?" Dad asks, opening his eyes to search mine.

Way to lob a loaded question.

Do I want to go? Honestly, no. Spotlight, attention, cameras, and crowds are not my scene. But along with that rainbow-and-ponies fantasy of Mom and me skipping off into the sunset, I still want answers about my past, and the only way to get them may just be to step inside Caterina's world. Be around her more than just a few brief moments so I can decipher truth from fiction. Person from persona.

So, I say, "Why not? It could be fun."

I feel the weight of Lucas's stare on my cheek, but I don't turn to meet it.

Dad hesitates before letting out a long breath. "All right. But I'm sending Jack with you."

Caterina nods, clearly understanding this isn't negotiable. Another weird silence falls, and I glance at Ransom. He hasn't said anything this whole time, just sat there silently watching and fiddling with his fork.

I wish I knew his story. Knew how he really felt about

our mother, and about me. Is he down for this whole togetherness gig, or is he as wary and confused as I am? Lucas doesn't trust him. Normally, that's *my* department. But when it comes to Ransom, I can't seem to find the energy. I understand the need to know your parents. To see where you come from and get answers about your past.

For the first time since he walked into the airport terminal, I look at him—really look at *him* and not the boy who looks like Cipriano or the rocker who seems so lost. He's nineteen years old, on his own, an adult who must have some kind of life back home. Yet he sought our mother, this spectacle, out for a reason. What is it?

What does he hope to gain?

Rance glances up and catches me staring. His dark eyes give nothing away. After a moment, I force a smile and take a bite of Jenna's chocolate cream pie. Maybe the answers lie in a sugar rush. Right now, it's about the best plan I've got.

Clue Number One

·*Lucas*·

I shove my wallet in the back of my jeans, grab my jacket and keys, then stare at the present I had made for Cat. I'm still debating on if I should take it. I may've talked big last night, and I like to think I can be romantic when need be, but I've never worked so hard for a girl in my life. Never put so much thought into a date or cared if the girl would like it. This gift could be either the sweetest Valentine's Day present ever or the lamest.

But hey, at least it's *real*.

Grounding Cat in reality is one of the things I hope to do tonight…that and exploring our PG-13 rating some more. Hearing her agree to go with her mom to that premiere threw me at lunch. The girl I know desires privacy and wants her art to speak for her. She prefers being behind the camera, taking pictures for her portfolio, or storing them up to sketch later. She'd never put herself on the other side on purpose. At least, I never thought she would.

The possibility that I don't know Cat like I've always assumed I did is driving me crazy—but I know that I *do*. Cat's not into the superficial game. This is about her chasing her answers, and I'm all for her doing that.

I'm just scared that she'll lose herself, the girl I know, in the process.

The chime on the house alarm dings, followed by male voices. Pocketing Cat's present, I head out my bedroom door, tugging on my leather jacket. I'd hoped that my father and his business partner wouldn't return until after I'd left. Seeing him this morning reminded me of Angela's suspicions. Dad moved here to get the L.A. office of Lirica Records running. That sort of thing takes time, and there should be no reason for us to move again. But, now that they're here, I may as well see what I can find out just in case. I'm halfway down the hall, ready to interrogate, when the sound of my father's laugh stops me in my tracks.

Holy shit.

It's rough and almost rusty, as if his throat forgot how to make the sound—but it's *his* laugh. I haven't heard it since David died, but I'd know it anywhere. It filled my childhood. It's infectious. It always inspired my mom's beautiful smile and then her tinkling laughter, and soon, we'd all be laughing, even if we didn't know why. A knot settles thick and hard in my stomach as my feet pick up speed. I need to prove with my eyes that I didn't imagine it. As I reach the living room, the sound breaks again.

"Dad?"

My father looks over from his conversation with his partner, and the knot jumps into my throat. Dad's eyes... they're not dead. They're also not shining with joy and humor, like they used to do when he laughed. But it's an improvement. Angela looks over her shoulder at me, and I see the same curiosity and fear reflected on her face.

We want our dad well. Hell, we want our dad *back*.

But why is he coming back to us *now*?

"Lucas, we were just talking about you," my father says, instantly making my spine lock.

Mr. Rossi smiles at me. "Your dad was catching me up on how you and your sister have been fairing here in the States. Sounds like you found your place. Still the soccer star."

Of course. That's all I am to my dad. Not the artist guy, or the guy who loves cars, but the soccer player. The stand-in for David.

Resentment that's been boiling for months—years— rises to the surface, agitated by suspicion. Angela's right— every move we've made has been preceded by a visit like this. Like hell Mr. Rossi's simply here for meetings. He's here to screw with my world.

"I have found my place, sir," I say, hurt and adrenaline fueling my need to get it all out, once and for all. "But not on the field. Soccer's not really my thing anymore."

Angela's dark head whips around, *Exorcist*-style, from her spot on the sofa. Mr. Rossi jerks in surprise, and Dad's non-dead but not joyful eyes flash with fire. Two distinct reactions, emotions, from him in one day. That's a damn record.

My sister's wide-eyed gaze grabs mine as she mouths, "*Now?*"

She's right. I don't have time for this. I need to make sure everything is set for my date, and then I have to pick up Cat. This is the worst possible time to have this discussion, and I don't need to say everything now. But I'm not going another second pretending to be someone I'm not—especially when I fear Cat's in danger of doing the same thing.

"Since when is *soccer* not your thing?" my father asks. He glances at his partner, and I sense his inner battle. Maybe he's right. Maybe this shouldn't happen with an audience. But thank Christ it's finally happening.

"It's never been my thing," I confess, a weight lifted from my chest as I say the words I've wanted to say for three years. "If you ever really saw *me,* you'd know that. Soccer was David's sport. I did it to hang out with him, because I idolized my big brother. And then when he died, I played it to please you. But I'm over it, Dad. I'm through with living my life for someone else. Come Monday, I'm telling Coach I want off the team."

Ignoring Dad's sharp intake of air, and my own inner desire to lay it all on the table now, to tell Dad that if he moves back to Milan, he'll be doing it without me, I begin walking again. A smile twitches my lips as I cross the living room. Let him think on this tonight; then we'll talk.

Angela's eyes and mouth are open so wide she looks like a Picasso painting, but I feel almost weightless as I pass her. Euphoric. Eager for the future. Oh, there's a little scared shitless in the mix, too, but I'll worry about Dad's reaction when I get home.

Right now, I have a date.

• • •

The rumbling of my bike catches the neighbors' attention, along with my paparazzi friend, as I pull into Cat's driveway. I lift two fingers in a wave, still unable to believe I talked Mr. Crawford into letting his daughter ride with me. Understandably, he's concerned. Owning a motorcycle isn't nearly as common here as it is in Italy, and the guy is super protective. He made me jump through a few hoops last night, and I had to bring my safe driving certificate this morning. What really sold him on it was my vow to let Jack tail us—that and his belief that Cat needs this. Something unexpected and fun. With all the ways the world is rapidly changing around us this week, a motorcycle ride seems tame.

Plus, he threatened me within an inch of my life if I even thought about going over forty-five. Or touch a drop of anything liquid other than water.

Shoving my hands in the pockets of my jeans, wondering why I suddenly feel so nervous, I hike up to the door. Jack and his partner nod as I walk past their truck. They're punctual bastards; I'll give them that. But honestly, as much as it sucks having chaperones on Valentine's Day, I don't mind the security detail so much. They keep their distance when it's important, and my plans involve plenty of alone time. My blood heats as I knock.

"Prepared to swoon my ass off," Cat says in lieu of *hello* when the door swings open. She winks and then twirls around, showing off her outfit. All I told her was that she needed to be ready at five, and to wear jeans and her leather jacket. The jacket is draped across her arm, the jeans are molded to her curves, and her silky top is dark blue, setting off her gorgeous eyes. "Is this appropriate mystery date attire?"

I lean in to kiss her lips, glad to see her smile. I've been on cloud nine since I finally put it on the line and stood up to my father...but seeing Cat happy, knowing what I have planned, and watching her take the night of surprises in stride shoots it to another level.

"Perfect," I say, nipping at her lip. "You look edible."

She laughs and rolls her eyes, but her cheeks glow a bit brighter. "Flattery will get you everywhere, though since you're a guy, I'm betting you're just hungry." She sticks her head back through the door and calls out, "Love you!" then closes it firmly behind her. "Do I at least get a tiny hint about tonight?"

I take her jacket and hold it out, helping her slip her arms through the holes. Grasping her shoulders, I spin her around and let her see my bike waiting in the drive. "Clue number one."

Cat squeals and does a bounce-like dance. "Are you serious?" She shoots me a quick, questioning look, and when I nod, her face becomes a mask of confusion and eagerness. "Did you clear it with Dad first?"

"You think I'm stupid, woman?" I wrap my arms around her slender waist, imagining how it'll feel having *her* arms wrapped around mine. And thighs straddling my hips. I glance at the photographers snapping away near the fence, and immediately begin thinking about puppies. "Of course I cleared it with him. As if I could get away with *not* clearing it between your bodyguards and *Star* magazine staked outside your door."

"Touché," she says before doing another bounce step. "I'm gonna ride a motorcycle. That's so badass!"

I chuckle and link our fingers, tugging her forward. "Come on, little badass. Let's give the paparazzi something worth capturing."

Her answering smile is so dazzling it nearly steals my breath. Knowing I put it there makes me feel like a freaking king. "Are you trying to get me in trouble, Mr. Cappelli?"

"Always, Miss Crawford," I reply. "Always."

With a knowing nod at the bodyguards as we approach my bike, I remove my second helmet from the seat and help her put it on, smoothing back her hair and strapping it. I step back and look at her. Standing beside my bike in curve-hugging denim and leather, the black helmet in place, she does look like a badass. *My* badass. And she's never looked hotter.

"Damn, I wish I could kiss you right now." Both the helmet and the prying eyes of the paparazzi keep that from happening, but when I catch her licking her lips in response, I groan and shove on my own helmet. "The quicker we get where we're going, the better."

Her eyes light up from behind the visor as I flip it down. I hop on my bike and take her hand, tugging her close. "Swing your leg around and scoot up close."

Cat does as I say, intuitively grabbing onto my hips and pulling herself closer. She's not close enough. She'll never be close enough, but I take her hands and lace them around my stomach, then grasp her knees and tug them firmly beside mine. She slides an extra inch. The scent of leather and rose mingles in my nose as the heat of her body seeps past the denim. I could get used to this.

I look back to see her face. Her flirty grin says she's enjoying this as much as I am. "During a turn, you're gonna lean slightly. When we turn right, look over my right shoulder, and keep your body in line with mine. When we turn left, look left. Got it?"

She lowers her gaze to where my lips are behind the visor and shifts closer. "Look and lean. Got it." Her voice is a mixture of excitement, fear, and desire.

This was an excellent idea.

"One more thing?" I say, waiting for her gaze to flutter back to mine. "Hold on tight and enjoy the ride."

Cat laughs, and pressed up against me like she is, I feel the vibrations throughout my body. I yank the clutch, press the starter, and feel her jerk behind me as the engine rumbles to life.

"Best Valentine's Day ever!" she screams in my ear.

And it's only just begun.

·Cat·

Riding wrapped around Lucas's firm body as the world blurs in a whirlwind of color and sound might just be the highlight of my existence. At the very least, it makes my top ten moments. Our speed is slow as Lucas navigates us through the streets of my neighborhood, but it doesn't matter. Even with the obviously Dad-approved pace, this is nothing short of exhilarating.

With a tummy full of butterflies and white noise in my ears, I can't think about my mother and brother. I can't stress, wondering if by wanting to know them better, I'm somehow hurting Dad and Jenna. On the back of Luc's bike, all I can do…all I *want* to do…is feel.

From this viewpoint, Wilshire Boulevard looks brand new. I've traveled this road more times than I can count, but today feels like the first. The scenery is different. Palm trees are taller, the street somehow bigger. The colors of the buildings are crisper. I snuggle into Lucas's back, loving the sensation of being so close and wishing I wasn't wearing this dang helmet so I could get even closer. Wishing that I could stay right here in this moment of not doing, but simply *being*, forever.

When Lucas takes a right onto Comstock, I have an inkling where he's taking me. Holmby Park is on this street, a beautiful spot with walking paths and tons of trees. It would be a great place to kick off our date. But I'm not ready to end the ride.

Lucas slows as we near the four-way stop near the park, and I sigh…only then to release a completely random (and *un*-Cat-like) giggle when he shoots right past it. The muscles of his taut stomach shake with his laugher, and I close my eyes as I grin. I don't need to see where we're going. I don't really care where he takes me or what we do. As long as we're together, and away from the insanity of home, I know it'll be amazing.

All too soon, however, the exhilarating ride does end. This time when the bike slows a few minutes later, it feels legit, and when it comes to a full stop and Lucas puts down the kickstand, I reluctantly pry open my eyes. A row of gnarly trees, tall buildings, and a cool, funky sculpture greets me. I glance around, trying to get my bearings, and see a sign directing university vehicles.

"Where are we?"

"UCLA," Lucas replies, hopping off. He slides his hands around my waist and lifts me up, and for a moment, I'm completely weightless.

That's hot.

He sets me on my feet and takes off his helmet, shaking out his golden curls before removing mine. Caressing my hair to smooth what I'm sure is crazy helmet hair, he grins down at me with an expression bordering on vulnerable.

That's even hotter.

"This place is important to me," he says with a slight shrug. "I wanted to share it with you. Before my family moved back to Milan the last time, we used to live just up the road. Whenever the day was nice, Mom would pack a lunch and bring us here."

I look around again, seeing the scenery through his young eyes. Something tugs inside my chest.

Lucas is my first real boyfriend. That makes today my first *real* Valentine's Day—the first one that didn't just involve gifts from my dad anyway. Even while excited, I've been nervous about tonight, too, not knowing what to expect. After debating all afternoon, I figured it would be some variation of the old movie and dinner routine.

But this?

Taking me to an important place and sharing a part of himself? That's the stuff romantic comedies are made of… and it makes me want Lucas even more.

I didn't think that was possible.

Lucas clears his throat. "Anyway, Mom was an artist, too. She and my dad actually met here, at UCLA. Officially, she got an accounting degree, but her minor, and her heart, was in art. She passed that on to me, I guess, by bringing me to her favorite place." He looks toward the gnarly trees. "The Murphy Sculpture Garden."

He shrugs again and shifts on his feet, obviously nervous,

and I want to tackle him to the ground. I'm completely, 100 percent falling for this guy, and he has no clue how wonderful he is. How special. That feeling tugs my chest again, driving home the reason I'm doing this thing with my mom. Why I have to see it through. If I have any hope of becoming the kind of girl Lucas deserves, I *need* to get closure. When I finally say those three little words and give my heart to this beautiful boy, I want it to be whole.

Sliding my hand into his, I say honestly, "This is perfect, Luc."

"Yeah?"

He searches my eyes with a crooked grin, and I nod. "Yeah. I couldn't think of a better place for our date."

That crooked grin grows until it reveals his lethal dimple. "Well then, you should know the ride and a picnic is only phase one of my plan." A mischievous glint lights his chocolate-brown eyes. "Plenty more surprises still to come." Squeezing my fingers, he pulls me forward until I'm standing right in front of him, and he leans down to kiss the tip of my nose. "Follow me, little badass."

Proving just how little I know about motorcycles, I'm shocked as he quickly removes a pouch from the side of his bike. When he unzips it to look inside, I peek and notice it does indeed hold a picnic dinner, as well as a blanket. He catches me before I can see what else it holds, however, and tucks the bag beneath his toned arm.

"All will be revealed in time," he intones, mimicking Reyna's mysterious accent.

I laugh. "Gosh, you're a dork." But I wrap my arms around his waist and hug him tight, letting him know I'm only teasing. I love that he knows about my gypsy girl and my fantastical/impossible journey to the past. Sharing it with him reminds me how lucky I am.

Lucas presses his lips to the crown of my head, and I'm tempted to stay here, just like this. But I can feel Lucas twitching, antsy to show me his favorite spot, so I step back. "Lead on, Professor."

His smile is infectious as he takes my hand, and I find myself hanging on every word as he leads me down the sidewalk and begins explaining the sculptures that shaped his childhood.

As I listen to him talk, I catch a glimpse of the young boy who fell in love with creation.

Being here with him, soaking this place in, I totally get the inspiration. My fingers literally twitch with the urge to sketch. To capture the beauty, the tranquility, the brilliance of this park on paper. For now, I settle for snapping picture after picture with my cell phone, storing up memories so I can attempt to recreate them at home.

"What I wouldn't give for a sketchpad," I murmur as we walk past a soothing fountain. The water trickles down from a funky sculpture, surrounded by tall trees, and for the first time in my life, I think about college. My future. I can see myself here.

I glance at Lucas and catch him looking at the ground with a small, satisfied grin.

When the sun begins to set behind the trees, he stops beneath a big, shady tree and spreads the blanket from his bag. It's been an amazing afternoon, with zero talk of our current family dramas—Lucas's rule. I snap another picture of him lying there, hair mussed, skin flushed from our walk. Maybe I'll sketch *him* later, too.

He rolls his eyes and holds up his hand. "All right, Annie Leibovitz," he says, referencing my favorite photographer. "Enough pictures. Join me."

Snagging my wrist, he tugs me onto the blanket as he sits up. After placing me between his open legs, my back to his chest, he releases a breath of contentment. I know the feeling. A few stragglers remain in the park, other than Jack and his partner, who I spy hanging out near the fountain. I'm sure there's a photographer or two hiding in the trees, too, hoping for a scandalous make-out scene. But I *feel* like we're alone. *Perfection.*

As vibrant colors streak across the sky, I say, "This is beautiful."

"Not as beautiful as you." He slides my hair to one shoulder and chuckles against my ear, sending chill bumps racing across my skin. "That sounds like a cheesy line I ripped from *Valentine's Day for Dummies*, but I happen to really mean it."

I smile, knowing he does. And that's what is so amazing.

I wiggle my hips back, snuggling into him, and Lucas presses his lips to my neck. A shiver rolls down my spine. To distract myself from turning around and giving the hidden paparazzi precisely what they want, I focus on a young mother and little girl a few feet away. The two of them are holding hands, the girl skipping, the mother smiling.

"Before I feed you," Lucas murmurs, his lips brushing my ear as he speaks. The resulting shiver now spreads to my toes. "I thought we could do something first."

At the tone of his voice, I tear my gaze from the sweet family moment and crane my neck around, wide-eyed. We're in public, with cute, innocent eyes within viewing distance…but still, I'm tempted. Lucas laughs when he sees my expression and promptly opens the saddlebag. Grinning, he whips out a box of drawing pencils and a sketchpad. "You didn't think I meant something else, did you?"

I shove his shoulder playfully—he knows *exactly* what I thought he meant. Shaking my head, I grasp his chin and pull him in for an eager kiss, then exclaim against his lips, "Dude, you flipping rock!" Now this date is officially perfect. I make grabby hands at the supplies. "Gimme."

His smile widens as he hands over the goods, and then he removes a second pad, presumably for himself. While I tend to gravitate toward sketching, painting, and photography, Lucas is more into sculpting and ceramics…but his talent knows no bounds. Having him in my art class fires up my competitive edge like nothing else (along with other *fiery* thoughts), and our teacher, Mr. Scott, loves our friendly rivalry. Ever since Lucas transferred in January, my portfolio has pretty much been made of win.

Tapping through my pictures, I land on the image of a cool female figure and begin to sketch. It doesn't take long to lose myself in capturing the piece. The fluid form of her body, the drape of her skirt. It's just a torso, no arms, no head, no legs. It's beautiful in its simplicity. But midway through, I sigh and flip the page, beginning a new drawing. This one featuring a little girl, eyes full of joy, and a mother beside her, smiling with loving pride.

For so long, I thought that kind of connection was a pipedream. That's why I got my tattoo, inspired from my favorite painting *Madonna and Child with Apples and Pears*, to remind me of that.

In the famous painting, Mary looks at her child with

such love and adoration—an expression my own mother never wore. On the table in front of her are an apple and two pears, one of them sliced in half. In Renaissance art, pears symbolize marital fidelity, which I always found fitting since my mother's infidelity sliced our family apart.

Somehow, a Renaissance artist captured my life story in paint five hundred years before it ever happened. And just a few years ago, I captured it somewhat illegally in ink on my hip—a sliced pear, a permanent reminder that the heart can't be trusted. That it only ever leads to pain.

At least that's what I used to believe. Thanks my ancestors and the beautiful boy beside me, my views have shifted. And with Mom suddenly wanting to be a part of my life, I can't help thinking that maybe she *will* look at me that way…someday. Even if she doesn't, even if it *is* just a pipedream, I owe it to the hurt little girl inside me to find out for sure.

I don't budge from my spot or lift my head until a shadow falls across my paper. When I look up, I realize the sun has all but set, the colors deep and vibrant on the horizon. Lucas watches me with a wistful smile on his face, and I can tell that he's seen my sketch. That he understands. I lower my lashes and close the pad, stretching and massaging my stiff neck. It's not that I'm embarrassed that he knows; it's just still new for me to be so exposed.

Lucas takes my drawing hand and presses a soft kiss against my knuckles. "Would you like to see my sketch?" he asks, smoothly shifting the focus away from me.

Grateful, I nod, eager to return to the land of happy, swoony thoughts. "I'd love to."

He hands over his work, and I expect to see a cool car

or maybe the stainless steel cross that he seemed to love so much. When I look at the paper, however, my head tilts in confusion.

It's a flower.

A beautiful flower, don't get me wrong. But…a flower.

Definitely not the manliest of things to draw. I think back, trying to remember if we saw any rosebushes on our walk, but I come up blank. Scrunching my nose, I ask the obvious. "Why a rose?"

He beams, as if he'd been waiting for me to ask that very thing. *O-kay.*

"Did you know that in Renaissance art, a rose with eight petals symbolizes renewal?"

His gaze flickers down, toward my hip, and a lump forms in my throat. I swallow it down, my earlier thoughts still fresh in mind. Tears prick my eyes as I return my gaze to the sketch and count eight petals.

"No," I whisper. "I didn't know that."

"You told me the story about your tattoo," Lucas says, sliding closer to me on the blanket. "And I know what it represents. Or what it used to represent. I'm hoping that maybe your opinion has changed in the last few months. Since you went to the past and met Alessandra." He pauses, and I lift my head to meet his eyes. "Since you met me."

I nod again, that lump back in my throat, making words impossible.

A smile curves his lips as he searches my face and seems to find what he's looking for. Leaning back, he slides his hand into his pocket. "I thought you could use a new reminder. Not necessarily in ink, but one close to your heart…and possibly just as permanent."

Confused, I look down and see him fingering a small suede pouch. My pulse begins to race as he turns it over, spilling a silver chain into his opened palm. A tear escapes when I see the charm sitting on the end.

An eight-petal rose.

"May I?" he asks, lifting the delicate chain.

I nod, still unable to speak, and scoot so he can clasp it around my neck. When the cool, soft weight touches my skin, my heart stutters beneath the charm.

Lucas presses a kiss at my nape and slips his arms around me. "Cat, I understand your need to explore the possibilities with your mom." His voice is low and gentle in my ear, and another tear falls. "But never forget that you're already loved. Unconditionally. Chase whatever you need to find, get your closure. But whatever way this turns out, know that it doesn't affect *us*. There's no need to fear me leaving or ever hurting you."

I close my eyes as his words flow over me.

There's a difference between loving someone and being *in* love with them. I know that, and I'm not sure which one Lucas means. But he does care for me, deeply, and that truth fills me with so much joy I could burst.

A strange sensation flutters in my chest—almost as if a piece of my heart is healing. Another section of the puzzle I've been building these last few months is stitching itself back together. I turn in Lucas's arms, and although I'm unable to return his sentiment now—I can't promise something that isn't yet fully mine to give—I do my best to show him how I feel. If not with words, then at least with my lips.

He seems to get the message.

Groaning, Lucas thrusts his fingers through my hair and holds me still, devouring my mouth for one wonderful, glorious minute. His lips are soft, yet firm, and when his tongue flicks out to lick the seam of my lips, I open eagerly, wanting more. Almost needing it.

But more never comes.

"What the hay?" I grumble, nipping his lower lip when he pulls back.

He rests his forehead against mine and exhales heavily. "The trees have eyes," he reminds me, referring to our friendly photographic friends.

I grumble again, knowing he's right. We can't get carried away—as much as I really, *really* want to. Not so much because the world would see pictures of Lucas and me making out on the cover of some tabloid…but because my *dad* would see it.

That reality pours more cold water on my libido than a freaking tsunami.

Lucas chuckles at my expression as he stands and gently takes my hands to lift me up. "Don't worry. I have the perfect place in mind where no one will see us." He wags his eyebrows, and a spark of mischief enters his eyes, making me laugh. "Prepare for phase two."

• • •

I frown as I gaze at the abandoned warehouse. We're in a deserted part of town I've never been in before, there's a broken-down car a few feet away with a busted-out windshield, and almost every streetlight on the block is out.

Phase two is looking pretty shady about now.

"You're right, no one will see us here," I agree with a slow nod and pop of my hip. "And there's a very good reason for that." I look at him and circle my finger in the air. "This place is condemned."

Lucas shakes his head as he yanks out his keys and proceeds to unlock the main door to the building as if he owns the joint. The fact that he has keys to this suspect place is both intriguing and a bit terrifying.

"It's not condemned," he says, grunting as he twists the key in the stubborn lock. It gives, and he glances back with a satisfied smile. "But it *is* private. Come on, where's my little badass?"

"On a momentary siesta," I mutter, lifting to my toes. I try to sneak a peek past his shoulder, although to be honest, I'm kind of scared of what I might see.

Lucas chuckles. "Wait here. I'll be right back."

He widens his eyes with excitement, then disappears through the opened door before I can say *heck no*. I glance over at Jack, parked in his truck and reading a newspaper. Said security man lifts his head as if he can feel my anxious stare, then sends me a wink through the windshield.

If Dad's main guy thinks this is legit, it must be. *Right*?

Before I can answer my own question, the door to the building opens and Lucas returns. "Everything's ready."

The naked bulb suspended over the doorway reveals his vulnerable smile from the park is back, mixed with anticipation. He tries to hide his eagerness, but his hands are tapping his thighs, and his neck is doing this adorable chicken jut thing. It completely wins me over. Despite the heebie-jeebies bouncing like Pop Rocks in my gut, I give him my hand and close my free one around my new delicate charm, choosing to follow him. To let him tug me into the great and nerve-wracking unknown.

Inside the rusted-out door is a sea of pitch black. Lucas releases my hand to flick on the overhead light, and I blink at the sudden change. When my surroundings come into focus, my gasp echoes in the wide, deserted space.

A huge blank canvas lines one wall. Tarps cover the entire floor. And tubs of what appear to be balloons filled with some kind of substance sit in intervals along the ground.

"No. Way." I turn to my amazeballs boyfriend in shock. "Are you a closet *Princess Diaries* fan?"

Lucas laughs, a deep, rumbly sound, and tucks a section of hair behind my ear. "No, but Angela is," he says. "I'm not too proud to admit I hit up my little sister for advice. And since she knows we both love art, she suggested this from her favorite movie. As for this place, an old friend of my mom's owns it." He glances at the tub of balloons I now know contain paint, and then back at me. "Dumb idea?"

"*Awesome* idea," I correct. I look down at my pretty top and frown. "Although I probably should've worn an old tee for this."

Lucas taps my chin up and winks. "Got you covered, babe." He walks over to the nearest tub and grabs two plastic raincoats I hadn't noticed. "Literally covered."

He grins at his bad pun and helps me slide on my coat. The plastic crinkles as I twist my hair into a ponytail and shove it under the hood. He did well—the coat must be ogre-sized, because it covers me from head to foot. I kick off my pretty shoes just in case and snap the buttons closed, doing a happy shimmy. I've always wanted to try this.

"Rules," he declares, picking up one of the balloons.

"There are no rules. The balloons are divided into tubs of red, blue, yellow, purple, and green paint. You lob those suckers at the canvas, the balloons explode, and magic happens."

He widens his eyes theatrically, and I shake my head, imagining the work he must have done to put all this together. "Wow," is all I can say.

Lucas's smile widens and he brings his elbow back like he's aiming for my head. He laughs at my scowl and says, "Ladies first."

Rubbing my hands together, I survey my options. The first dab of paint on a clean canvas is always the most exciting. A new beginning that sets the tone. I decide on purple, the color of royalty (a nod to the character who inspired this date), and pitch it at the wall.

Color explodes in a burst of vivid orchid, and I slap my hand over my mouth.

That felt amazing.

"This is an excellent stress reliever," I declare, picking up a yellow one and heaving it next. The contrasting colors are so bright, so beautiful in their dissent…so messy on the canvas. So unlike anything I've ever done.

My art is like me—controlled. Portraits, landscapes, photorealism. I don't think I even colored outside the lines when I was a kid. But breaking the rules like this—with *Lucas*—is fun.

All traces of earlier nervousness now gone, Lucas grins as he picks up a red balloon. He winds back, and even through the clear plastic coat, I see the muscles of his bicep bunch. His weight shifts, and aiming for the clean side of the canvas, he lobs the paint at the wall. I sigh.

Why watching that was sexy, I don't know. It just was.

After that, we go at it, lobbing color after color at the canvas, laughing and taunting each other. It's silly, and we're having fun, two things I definitely didn't expect when Lucas picked me up on his motorcycle. Or when he stopped outside what looked to be a location for a horror film. But this is exactly what I needed.

Lucas gets me.

Soon the canvas is completely covered, colors blending in new shades, all of it one big blob. I haven't become a converted abstract artist during this exercise, but I know with everything in me that I'll be doing this again.

Lucas swipes a red balloon and tosses it in the air. When he catches it, he grins.

"You look way too clean over there," he declares, his voice heavy with disapproval. His gaze skims over my pristine coat, and I follow suit. It's true, not a drop of color is on me. He, on the other hand, squeezed a few balloons too hard and paint exploded all over him.

"Guess I'm just good like that," I say with a shrug. Being totally type A doesn't hurt, either.

"Oh, you're definitely good." Lucas's left arm shoots out and snags my waist. "But unless you get some on you, I'm not sure you've experienced the true spontaneous spirit of balloon art."

"Spontaneous spirit?" I palm the blue balloon he's yet to see behind my back and smile with innocence. "You think I need to be more spontaneous?"

He nods, and the action knocks back his hood. I eye his golden curls as he leans down to brush his lips against mine once, twice, and then says against my mouth, "Yes, I'd— "

Before he finishes that thought, I smash my balloon over

his head.

Of course, some paint splatters on me, too, but it's *so* worth the utter look of confusion and shock that washes over him.

Blue paint oozes in his curls, and rivulets trickle down the sides of his tanned face. I laugh, loving that for once *I* was the one doling out the surprises...then gasp as Lucas pushes back my hood and slams *his* paint balloon over the back of *my* head.

Thick, cool liquid gushes over my unprotected hair. I squeeze my eyes shut in case any makes its way toward them, then shiver as goose pimples prick the back of my neck at the odd, icky sensation. Lucas's mouth slams against mine, hot, eager, and passionate, and those goose pimples multiply *everywhere*.

Scooping me up, his mouth never leaving mine, he shifts his hands to my bottom. He lifts me until I wrap my legs around his plastic-covered hips, then palms the back of my paint-coated head, kissing me with an urgency I've never experienced before.

Making me feel wanted in a way I never thought I would.

My arms latch around his neck, and I hang on tight. I match Lucas stroke for stroke, nibble for nibble, as we pour all the fun, all the excitement, all the *romance* of the day into the kiss. And as the hour of my Cinderella-like curfew draws closer, I try and show Lucas just how much feeling *wanted* means to me.

Secrets and Lies

·Cat·

My fashionista friend is parked at my locker bright and early on Monday, two Venti Caramel Macchiatos in hand, eyes wide and eager for details. Details that have been piling on since Hayley and I last saw each other at Jenna's aborted bachelorette party—the day my world went wonky.

Accepting the much-needed caffeine jolt with a muttered, "Thanks," (morning person I'm not), I gulp the delicious beverage as my mind trips over the events of the past few days. The scene at the airport, the awkwardness at The Ivy. The discomfort of family lunch, followed by the best Valentine's Day in history. Where do I even begin? Luckily, Hayley's paper-thin patience wears out before I can decide, and what I'm sure is the first of the day's questions begin:

What is Caterina *really* like? (Answer: the jury is still out.)

Is it true major sparks flew between her and Dad on Saturday? (Answer: Uh, no, not unless by *sparks* you mean ocular hate missiles.)

Is my new brother as sinfully hot in person as he looks on television? (Answer: Ew. And also, probably.)

When am I going to see either of them again? (Answer: Thursday.)

"Does Ransom have a girl—" Hayley cuts off midquestion. "What's Thursday?"

I quickly fill her in on the Holly Underhill premiere and my subsequent need to be beautified, after which she nods, shifts her gaze to the left, and firmly declares, "I'm on it."

This, as it turns out, is an understatement.

Two days later, Hayley shows up at my house as promised, dress in hand, shoes to match, and with serious thoughts as to how I should wear my hair. I point her in Jenna's direction, since that is her domain, and the two of them sit on the sofa, flipping through magazines for the next hour. It's the first and only time my future stepmother has looked excited about this whole thing.

Feeling strangely guilty, I turn away, lift the plastic protecting the dress, and trail my fingers along the silky material. It's gorgeous. Purple, fitted, sleeveless, and fancier than anything I've ever worn. Or even considered wearing, to a star-studded premiere or otherwise. It looks like something a model would wear—not a slightly awkward, attention-phobic chica, pretending she belonged. But it suits the situation, and I imagine it will make Caterina happy. Maybe even proud.

Some twelve hours later, as the scent of cooked hair fills the bathroom, my attention returns to the dress hanging on the back of the door.

"We'll just turn down the setting a bit," Jenna says. She gingerly touches an index finger to the long section of my hair wrapped around a curling iron. Her lips purse as the smooth skin around her focused eyes tenses.

It doesn't take one of those Big Bang nerds to see that she's stressing.

"It's looking good."

She lifts her gaze in question, and I circle my finger around my head like a halo. Ringlets she's assured me will be finger-combed and bunched in an elaborate style lie in a crazy array atop my head. Right now, the effect screams poodle, but I'm aiming to lighten the mood.

Jenna throws me a bone (pun intended) and offers a small smile.

It doesn't reach her eyes.

It's been like this ever since she signed me out of school this morning. Jenna being Jenna—sweet and enthusiastic— only an amplified version. She took me to lunch, feigned excitement over the celebrities rumored to show, and commented on all the *fun* I'll have tonight. But it's what she *hasn't* said that is working my last nerve.

I hear the sighs when she thinks I'm not paying attention. See the subtle winces she tosses my dress. When she mentions how bored she and Dad will be all night, how they'll be ready to go at a moment's notice, you know, if anything should happen…I infer what *anything* means. They don't think I'll fit in. They expect my mother to fail me somehow. And what I hate the most is that their doubts are starting to sink in.

If that weren't enough to get my hands quaking in my lap, the emotional tug of war over Jenna's help clinches it. Even with her apparent misgivings, she's been super supportive, taking off work to get me ready, doing my nails and makeup, styling my hair.

All the things a real mom does.

I flinch at the latest guilt-tinged thought, and Jenna notices.

Her gaze flicks to my reflection in the mirror as she slowly unravels a spiral of hair. Putting down the curling iron, she clamps her lips and grabs a can of hairspray, as if she's caging the words inside. Words I know are just dying to bust out.

She aims the gold can, but before attacking my tresses, she opens her mouth, closes it, then tries again. "It's not too late, you know."

And there it is.

I knew it was coming, but I still exhale in frustration. Why does no one understand this? Lucas comes the closest, but even he doesn't get why I *need* to do this. Not totally. Anger joins the potent mix of guilt, confusion, and frustration already roiling in my gut, and through clenched teeth, I ask a question I already know the answer to. "*What's* not too late?"

Jenna shifts her weight. "Tonight." She clears her throat and sets down the can. "Sweetheart, listen, I understand wanting to know your mother. I do. And I think it's great that she's come back and wants to spend time with you, too. It's just that…this premiere, the photographers and crowd. It's not exactly your scene." She winces as she says it, and my eyes close with a laugh. It's not funny, but that's what comes out anyway.

She's right. Tonight is so far from my scene, it may as

well be another movie. But the very fact that Jenna knows this and my own mother *doesn't* just adds fuel to the fire.

Caterina left when I was five. She never called or sent me a birthday card. She certainly never invited me to a premiere or an event. If she had, she'd know that I don't like this stuff, either. But she's here now. She *did* invite me this time. And if I back out, if I say no or admit I'm not the daughter she obviously thinks I am, who knows when she'll invite me again.

Backing out isn't an option. I have to do this, whether it's my scene or not.

Eyes still closed, emotions bubbling, I shake my head. "Maybe you don't know me like you think you do."

The words come out harsh. Much harsher than I intended. Opening my eyes, I see unmistakable hurt flare in hers, right along with the genuine concern always there. I glance away, pretending I don't notice either.

"People change," I say, even though I don't really believe that. People learn more about themselves all the time, they realize they like things they didn't know they did, or were mistaken about something important. But *true*, soul-deep change is rare.

Brushing that thought aside, I continue sharply, "And it just so happens I've *liked* the attention this week. For once, I'm not invisible."

That last part isn't total crap. Between photographers infiltrating school, students posing as my best friends to reporters, and receiving a bazillion and a half invites to upcoming parties, *invisible* is the last thing I've been.

From the corner of my eye, I watch Jenna's reflection as she gnaws on her lip. "Oh, well, that's good. Being visible is good. And hey, I'm in public relations. There's nothing wrong with liking a little attention."

Unless liking it goes against everything you've ever known.

In my world, attention has always meant unmet expectations. Whispers and cruel taunts. Jokes made at my expense and vicious rumors. I have the right pedigree, but I've never had a clue how to use it. This week has been one big learning curve.

On Monday, Desiree gave me notes for a class I missed. Yesterday, Lana smiled at me in Spanish. And this morning, Ray Thomas, one of the most popular guys in school, winked at me in the hall. It didn't hold a candle to Lucas's wink or sexy grin, but still. He *winked*. At me.

It's been like a bizarre scene straight out of *The Host*.

Alessandra thinks it's an intriguing sociological development. Lucas...well, Lucas isn't a fan. He believes popularity is fake, celebrity is a game of pretend, and all of it is fleeting. A week ago, I believed that, too. But that was before my world shifted. Now I'm realizing that game of pretend puts food on my table. My wanderlust mother thrives in the whirlwind of celebrity and popularity, and my father's films feed it. For the past few months, I've been searching for my place in the world.

Maybe *this* is it.

Jenna lets out an audible breath and shifts to stand in front of me. Folding her arms, she leans back against the counter. "Cat, I just want you to know that if you're having second thoughts, about tonight or anything else, it's okay." She smiles her Jenna smile, still not getting it. Not getting *me*. "If you want, you can even blame me for backing out."

The look in her eyes says it's a given that I'm not going anymore. Everything I've said about changing, about supposedly liking the attention, went straight in one ear and out the other.

Like everything else I've said since the Kate Lyons debacle last week.

Suddenly, it's all too much. The no one understanding. The walking on eggshells around Dad and Jenna, even Lucas and Less, not wanting to seem *too* eager, or naïve. The illusive answers and closure I need just out of my reach… It reaches its limit.

Emotions that have had no outlet until now find one. They boil to the surface, and I don't know how to stop them. I don't even *want* to stop them. I need to vent, to get all of the crap that's been clouding my chest and head out of me—and Jenna is just the unfortunate one who has ripped off the lid.

"You're not listening," I say, gripping the sides of my chair. "I don't want out of tonight. Caterina expects me there." A lock of curled hair falls in my face, and I blow it away. "And *she's* my mother."

I never say, "Not *you*." But the words seem to hang in the air as if I did anyway.

Jenna flinches, and my momentary adrenaline spike crashes. What light remained in her eyes fades, and I close mine, silently calling out to Reyna for a massive do-over. Jenna didn't deserve that. Especially not after helping me today. But as hard as I wish, no mystical bells chime. No mysterious wind envelops me. It's just Jenna and me, alone in an enormous marble bathroom smelling strongly of hairspray and cooked hair.

I open my eyes and let out a sigh. "Jenna, I didn't mean..." *Mean what?* I'm so exhausted right now, confused, I don't even know what I'm trying to say. Or do. I just want to stop feeling guilty, and for her to stop being hurt.

Jenna nods. "Don't worry about it." She forces a smile and surveys the mound of fresh curls on my head. "It's been enough chatter anyway. We need to get you ready! Caterina will be here any minute, and you're not even dressed."

With a touch more vigor than required, she gets to work combing through my curls. I know it can't be that easy. With Dad it would be; whenever we get in a disagreement, he goes off to watch sports, and five minutes later, the drama is forgotten. Girls are different—or so I'm learning. But the intent focus in Jenna's eyes as she gathers my hair in a cascading twist tells me to drop it. At least for now. With a guilt-laden, frustrated sigh, I scoot back in my chair.

The tune to an old Madonna song slowly fills the silence. It begins as a low hum, then builds to whispered sporadic lyrics. "Papa Don't Preach." It's Jenna's favorite, and she sings it cleaning, shopping, driving... Basically, the song's her anthem. I have no clue why. But as the familiar melody permeates the cloud of hairspray encircling my head, a small smile forms through the fog. It's so classic Jenna.

Four months ago, I never thought we'd be here. Getting along, doing my hair. I was convinced she was only out for Dad's money. For his fame and what he could do for her business. What *I* could do by having a televised sweet sixteen. But thanks to my trip to the past, I learned I was wrong. Jenna never misses a single parent-teacher conference or art show. She buys me supplies, she takes me to galleries, and she's even taking lessons of her own. She doesn't just make an effort—she follows through.

Jenna may not be my birth mother, but she's stepped up to fill the role in every sense that counts. She deserves better.

"Hey, Jenna?" I wait for her gaze to meet mine in the mirror and say, "Thanks for helping me today. You didn't have to, and I-I really appreciate it."

This time, her smile is quick, *real*, and full of forgiveness. "Just take a picture of Brad Pitt if you see him and we'll call it even, okay?"

· · ·

"Holy red carpet, Batman," I mutter, pressing my face against the tinted black window. We're a block away from the theater, and the crowd is already staggering. Flashes light up in the distance, the noise is deafening even from in here, and all I want to do is head back home to the safety of flannel pajamas. This isn't my first rodeo. I grew up going to premieres with Dad. But I don't remember it *ever* looking this crazy.

Caterina jostles my knee, and I turn to see her dazzling smile directed at me. "This is exciting, right? I knew it would be huge, but I think the fans came out in droves." She laughs lightly, like she has a secret. She notices me looking and leans in. "Ryan Seacrest had me on his show this morning. I was there doing general promo, you know, discussing what I have in the works, and I happened to mention the three of us were coming tonight. You should've seen the phone lines light up. The listeners went berserk!"

A rock settles in my gut, and my face must fall because her fluorescent smile dims.

"You don't mind, do you? I figured our attendance could create a little extra buzz for Marlena."

Marlena Adams is the world-famous director of the film, and Mom's good friend. They've done several movies and frequently show up together at events like this.

Is it weird that I'm jealous of an almost middle-aged woman?

"Of course I don't mind." I glance at Ransom, sitting across from me in his black tuxedo. He's rocked it out as much as possible—black on black, top two buttons undone, sunglasses hanging from his lapel. But watching his guitar pick seamlessly flow from one knuckle to the next, I can tell he's as jazzed about this public foray as I am. "We're glad to help."

My brother snorts under his breath. We still haven't gotten a chance to talk, *really* talk without our mom or camera-toting vermin listening in, but it's on my to-do list tonight. He's the one person out of all of this that may just understand. He's in the muck of it as much as I am. And the more time we spend together, the more this feeling of connection grows. Not the same kind I felt when I first saw Lucas, as if the universe was pointing in flashing neon, saying, "Look here! This guy is for you." This feeling is gentler, easier, *sisterly*. But no less real.

Caterina releases a relieved breath. "Good, I'm glad. I know this scene can be crazy at times. Living in a fish bowl. But it's really not all that bad." Reaching over, she takes my hand in hers. "Just be yourself out there, and you'll be fabulous. You're a natural, and they are going to love you."

It's as close as my mom has ever come to telling me the *L* word. A well of emotion builds in my sinuses, and I'm *this* close to ruining my makeup. I squeeze her hand, a wide smile breaking across my face, and say, "Thanks, Mom."

Her answering wink is so full of life and affection, I want to capture it on canvas and stare at it forever.

Then the limo rolls to a stop, and she tugs her phone out of her clutch. We're behind a few cars, but that doesn't stop the crowd from noticing us. As Caterina chats with whoever is on the other end—a publicist, manager, or one of her many minions—the attention starts. First, just a few heads turn. Then a dozen more. Questions come flying at our closed door, flashes go off, and I throw myself back into my seat.

Logically, I know they can't see me through the tinted windows…but try telling that to my skyrocketing pulse.

My stomach locks, my heart is in my throat.

Where the heck's a brown paper bag when you need one?

Resorting to the techniques they teach pregnant women in movies, I breathe through clenched teeth and pursed lips. "He, he, hooooo. He, he, hooooo."

I feel like an idiot. I have no clue if it's helping or not. But at least I'm no longer focused on the terrifying crowd. That's a plus.

"He, he, hoooo."

A negative would be Mom craning a dark eyebrow in my direction like I'm a wacko, but she just pats me on the knee and continues talking on her phone, as I continue breathing.

Rance scrunches his nose. "You all right there?"

I nod through the exhale. "Peachy."

He shakes his head at me, looking somewhat on board with the whole wacko thing, but his forehead relaxes, and he offers a small smile. Pocketing his pick, he glances at our mom. Then, leaning close, he says for my ears only, "I hate crowds, too."

I exhale again and tilt my head. "How can you be a performer and hate crowds?"

He shrugs. "When I play in bars, most of the time it's dark and smoky. I can't see anyone. Plus, no one's there for me anyway. I don't sing. I can just fade into the background, close my eyes, and play."

That is officially the most Ransom has ever said to me in one sitting. It also totally distracted me from my heaving stomach. I take a normal length breath, no alien-like sounds attached, and offer my brother a smile. "Guess we'll get through this together, huh?"

Rance lifts his chin as the limo inches forward again, and I spot a long white scar along his jaw. "You got it."

I think that counts as our first sibling bonding moment.

I want to ask about the scar. I'm tempted to push the moment and find out all I can about my brother. But now isn't the time. And it definitely isn't the place. Mom ends her call without saying good-bye and turns to us, eyes wide, smile megawatt. "Ready?"

No.

"Let's do this." I won't let her see me hesitate. I want her to be proud. Unbuckling, I slide closer to the window and wait as the driver strides toward my door. I rock my head side to side, roll my shoulders back, and give my brother a smile of solidarity. The door opens, and the screams hit me full-force like a tidal wave.

"Caterina!"

No, just plain old Cat, I want to say when I plant a heel onto the sidewalk. I take the driver's offered hand and push to my feet, pasting on the familiar smile I've worn all my life. No dimple, no nostril flare, zero weird eye crinkle. This is the public me. The only me anyone ever saw, other than Dad, up until a few months ago. It's strange that while it's easy to pull on, it now feels forced. I step to the side and let Ransom emerge. I notice his sunglasses are in place.

Immediately, my hands fly to my hips, then my bodice, and then my hair, as reality dawns. I forgot my sunglasses. How could this happen? Sixteen years of events like this, and I've *never* forgotten those suckers. I glance at the railing that keeps the surging crowd at bay. Swallowing hard, I feel my fake smile go manic.

Then, Caterina exits the car.

Hand in the air, she lifts her chin as she smiles and waves at her admirers like Miss America.

Flashes blind me (another reason sunglasses are so essential), and I attempt to hold my smile without flinching. It's about as easy as you'd think. I play it off as best I can and turn toward my brother. "A thousand bucks for those sunglasses."

I'm half teasing, and he must be able to tell because his lips turn up in a smirk. "No way. The rocker always gets the shades."

"Touché." My fake smile turns a bit more genuine—just a touch, since we are still in the midst of my own personal hell. But it's nice to tease Ransom. I imagine this is close to what normal feels like.

Four minions fall in place around us, and a woman wearing a headset and tailored suit steps in our path. "We're a happy family enjoying a movie together," she instructs, creeping me out with her use of *we*. And the fact that she's feeding us lines. Are we not really a family enjoying a movie together? Wasn't that the whole point?

"It's been a natural transition," she continues, walking backward on the red carpet and curling her fingers for us to follow. "We're glad for this chance to become a real family." She looks at Mom and says, "Motherhood is the greatest role there is."

Okay, this is seriously weird. Ransom shakes his head and adjusts his collar.

"Aren't they gorgeous?" My head snaps back as Caterina takes our hands and tugs us toward the railing on the right—the one for the media, and opposite the wall of ear-splitting chaos. A microphone with a giant six on it is thrust in her direction, and she says, "The two best things I've ever created."

Excuse me while I upchuck.

Guilt follows that thought, continuing my up and down ride of confusion. She's trying, in her own way, and this is what I wanted. Sort of. My mother holding my hand, claiming me, being proud of me. But something feels off. I also can't stop thinking about Jenna. How I lied and said this was now my scene. How I thought maybe this was where I belonged.

If this is what finding your place feels like, I think I'd rather be lost.

Reporters fire questions at the three of us, and Caterina lobs answers back without breaking a sweat. Sadly, I cannot say the same. Nonchalantly dabbing my upper lip with my fingers, I wipe at the collected moisture, give one-word responses, and think of my happy place. Lucas. Riding on the back of his bike. Throwing paint balls at the canvas. Kissing him in our paint-smattered coats, the blue and red combining to form my new favorite shade of purple.

When those thoughts bring heat to my cheeks—a predicament potentially just as embarrassing as sweating on camera—I look for another distraction and take a few small, subtle steps closer to Ransom.

"So," I say, angling toward his ear so he can hear me, "tell me your story."

He looks at me, then at our mother fielding questions in front of us. "Now?"

I shrug. Contrary to what I thought before, this may be the perfect time. It's not like anyone is really paying attention. Somehow, in the midst of the insanity, surrounded by hundreds, I feel more alone with Ransom than ever. "No time like the present. Besides, they don't care about us. We're just props for their video packages."

The truth of that statement stings, and yet it's also a relief. Rance frowns, considering it, then must decide I'm right. He doesn't appear that upset by the revelation, either.

We sidestep in line along the carpet as Caterina moves on to the next reporter, and over the sound of her rehashing our story yet again, my brother says, "What do you want to know?"

I think about it. "Honestly, everything. Everything and anything you want to share." I look at him and smile. "I've never had a brother before. You Googled me, so you know my story. Depending on how deep you dug, you know every embarrassing stumble, every zit, every bad fashion choice. I just want to know more than that you're in a band and…" I grin. "That abhorrence of attention may be genetic. Though clearly recessive, since it skipped our mother."

On cue, Caterina laughs at a joke and poses for another photo.

Ransom lifts his eyebrows at her and then shrugs. "I

graduated high school last year, went straight into college, and have no clue what I want to do. Other than music. When the fall semester ended, I told my folks I was taking off to focus on that."

My eyes widen in admiration. It's a familiar story, I'm sure. Guy into music drops out of school to play seedy bars and chase a dream and a lyric. But what I hear is that Ransom knows what he wants. He's found his place in the world, and all that's left is making it a reality.

"Did they flip out?" I ask, wanting to keep him talking.

"Dad didn't do a backflip, but he was all right. He's always encouraged my music. It's my mother who walked out of the room. But that's just Mom."

The harsh breath he releases tells me more than his words.

Filing that away for now, I move on to what brought him into my life. "And that led you here? Caterina said you were the one who reached out." I glance at the crowd, take another sidestep in line and smile at the latest reporter, then lower my voice. "Did you think she would help with your music? Get you connections?"

Ransom shakes his head before the questions are fully out. "Handouts don't get you taken seriously," he mutters, popping his knuckles. His jaw is tense, and I'm scared I offended him. But before I can apologize, he says, "I never even wanted to find her. She gave me up, she never tried to reach out… She could've gone to hell for all I cared."

Color me confused. "And yet you're here," I say, stating the obvious.

He slides me a look.

"What changed your mind?"

My brother stares ahead for what feels like forever. Caterina chatters on, turning and winking at us, pretending to include us in the conversation, and we move on to the next reporter. I don't know Ransom well enough to read the look on his face, and those dang sunglasses hide any clues he may be giving off.

Finally, he scratches the side of his jaw. "It's gonna sound unbelievable."

I laugh. I can't help it. "Trust me, I'm good with unbelievable. And implausible."

He drags his top lip between his teeth, considering, then shrugs in a way that seems to say, *why not.* "I've been staying with a friend in New York. My birthday was last month, and as a joke, he took me to see a psychic."

The noise around us silences as I turn fully to face him.

He gives me a weird look. "Yeah, total B.S., I know. But the girl was close to our age and she seemed cool. We had nothing better to do, so we went with it. Anyway, she read my tealeaves or whatever, and the whole time I thought it was a joke. But then out of nowhere she gave me some cryptic fortune about finding my *true* family."

Prickles of awareness creep down my spine.

"I couldn't shake it," he says, sounding confused. "I kept hearing her rough voice, nagging me to do it. Kept hearing Romanian words whispered around me. It was the weirdest thing, but finally I figured it couldn't hurt to try." He shrugs. "So I called up Dad, got Caterina's contact info from our lawyer, and here I am."

I look up at the night sky and repeat, "Here you are." I wink at the heavens and smile.

Reyna.

Suspicions

·Lucas·

So this is what people do when they don't have ass-kicking soccer practice every day. They watch mindless television. I have a paper due soon in English, a project to finish for Mr. Scott, and I could always head to the garage to mess with my bike. But this is nice. Doing nothing. Sitting next to my sister in a quiet house while she flips through the channels like a twitchy two-year-old hopped up on sugar.

"You realize there's such a thing as a menu, right?" I ask, amused by her restlessness. "And DVR?"

Angela nods, pausing for a fraction a second on Nickelodeon. A tall man in a bright orange jumpsuit sings with a boom box and strange-looking creatures. We look at each other and crack up laughing.

"Sure, but if we used that, we'd miss the joys of the

next generation," she says sagely, keying in the numbers for channel three and starting the process over again. "This way leaves room for surprises."

Surprises. A lazy smile crosses my lips as I think about Valentine's Day. Cat wrapped around me on my bike. Making out covered in paint. As nervous as I'd been about our date, it turned out better than I imagined.

A good thing, since we haven't seen much of each other this week.

Restless energy stirs inside me, and my leg begins to bounce. I check my phone again. Other than the brief glimpse of her in the halls, our only contact in the last twenty-four hours has been the selfie she sent of her crossed-eyed under a rat's nest of curls and the text saying she was ditching today. I wasn't surprised. In another move that proves just how clueless the woman is, Caterina kept Cat out until dawn. Mr. Crawford must've been spitting nails.

But now school is over, the weekend has begun, and other than that sunrise text, I haven't heard from my girl. When I called earlier, Alessandra answered and said she was still sleeping. I don't want to be *that* guy. The clingy, hovering one.

I check the time on my phone. Three o'clock.

I'll give it another hour.

Angela flips through the channels a few more times, and I catch a glimpse of a familiar smile. "Wait, go back."

She looks at me strangely but does it. When she lands on the channel I spotted, and sees the same frozen image, all she says is, "Oh."

A pretty blonde in a short dress and severe ponytail stands beside a photo of Cat's mom waving for the cameras.

I grab the remote and dial up the volume.

"Caterina Angeli made the rounds at the premiere for Holly Underhill's latest," she says. "The star-studded event had Hollywood's biggest celebs stopping by to show their support, but it was a certain brunette megastar's name that was on everyone's lips. Angeli graced the red carpet in support of good friend Marlena Powers, the film's director. And as she revealed to Ryan Seacrest on his radio show yesterday, her teenage children were in tow."

The video package goes on to show snippets of random celebrities commenting on Caterina being a mother. Older actors and actresses offer flat smiles and rattle off congratulations, but the younger ones are bolder.

"Crazy, right?" Jaycee Powers says, mouth gaping open. "Who knew she'd make such a great mother? The way she's taken her children under her wing and stepped up, that's just *so* great."

Reid Roberts, the teen actor who starred with Alessandra in the Shakespeare winter workshop, leans toward the camera next. He listens to the question and nods. "I actually met her daughter last month. She's a great girl. Gorgeous, too."

Angela smirks as I curse under my breath. I'd thought the guy turned out to be okay in the end, but maybe Austin was right after all. He is a douche.

The screen switches again to a shot of the two co-hosts against a backdrop of Los Angeles. An idiot with white Chiclets for teeth smiles at the blonde. "They sure do make a beautiful family, don't they, Krista?"

The woman nods enthusiastically. "They do indeed, Mark."

"Good Lord," Angela mutters.

Krista continues as the video switches once again to clips of the so-called beautiful family. "It's rumored that while at the after-party, Caterina met with producers about a possible new project. *It's a Quest* is in preproduction and already has a slew of big names attached. If Angeli joins that list, it will mark a decided shift for the box office favorite. Taking on the harried mother role instead of tempting vixen."

As she speaks, the video shows Caterina looking flawless as she loops her arms around Cat and Ransom. They walk down the red carpet, past the velvet ropes and a backdrop of film posters. Caterina's gaze remains glued to the crowd, her walk purposeful, as Ransom watches the ground and Cat stares straight ahead. She's stunning. Her dress flows over her curves, her hair is up, exposing the slope of her neck, and the sight of her punches me in the gut like it always does.

But the girl on the screen is not the girl who was on my bike Saturday. She's not the girl who hated having a televised sweet sixteen, or rolls her eyes at paparazzi. Her sunglasses are off, and she shares an amused smile with Ransom.

I don't even know this girl.

The host ends the segment by saying, "From the looks of things at the premiere, Caterina Angeli as a loving mother no longer seems so unrealistic. Sources say after her appearance last night, the role is practically hers."

And just like that, everything makes sense.

This is why she's here. This is the end goal I always knew existed but could never quite figure out. Caterina didn't come back to start an idyllic new life with her kids. Cat and Ransom are nothing but pawns in her stupid Hollywood game.

Thank God Cat's asleep right now.

As the hosts go on to talk about Holly and her costars,

along with the other big names that stopped by, I tell myself it'll be okay. Cat never watches this stuff, and right now, there's really no proof. It's all just speculation.

But that speculation is damning.

Projected opening box office numbers drone on as I feel Angela's stare on my cheek. "What are you thinking?" she asks me.

I swipe my hand across my face and throw my head back against the sofa cushion. "That the truth is going to destroy Cat."

. . .

An hour later, I'm calling again. I'm nervous that I'll slip about the show, but I need to hear Cat's voice. Need to ground myself in the girl I know and not the one I saw on television. As the call clicks over to voice mail, the door to my dad's office swings open.

I hadn't realized my parents were home.

Angela and I swap glances as the pair of them walk into the living room. Mom seems nervous. Maybe even more so than last week. Her hands are fisted, her lips moving subtly as if saying a string of prayers under her breath. Dad looks determined…and almost excited.

Real excitement requires effort, but since his meeting with Mr. Rossi, Dad has shown sparks of life. Interest in Angela's sweet sixteen, another shocking moment of laughter, and frustration and annoyance with me. We haven't spoken much since I told him I was off the team, but I've grown fluent in grunts.

"Good. Glad to see you both here." Dad's tone and expression are all business as he takes a seat in his favorite recliner. Mom settles for the padded armrest. She doesn't meet my eyes. "We have news we'd like to discuss with you."

Immediately, I know this isn't going to be good. Angela must think the same thing because she goes completely still beside me. Except for the pinky finger that snakes out to snag my own.

"As you know, Dario was in Los Angeles for meetings last week." Dad looks at me as he says this, clearly remembering how I dropped the *no soccer* bomb in front of his partner. "It seems that Lirica Records's last quarter has been busier and more profitable than expected. While I moved us back here to get the L.A. market running, I've kept my hands in everything occurring in Milan. With the surge of activity the last two months, it has been a challenge to manage both."

Dad waits for both of us to nod, acknowledging we're listening. I hear him, although I'm pretty sure I don't want to. The whole time he's been talking, Mom hasn't lifted her eyes from her lap. She just keeps smoothing nonexistent wrinkles from her linen pants. I swallow hard and turn back to Dad.

He rests his open hands on his knees. "Your mother and I realize it isn't easy uprooting lives on a whim. We asked a lot when we moved you at the end of last year, and we don't take asking you to do it again lightly. That's what we'd like to discuss now." His gaze darts between us. "Timing."

"Wait," I say, breaking free of Angela's tightened grip. I shake my head, clearly misunderstanding. "Are you saying it's already decided? No discussion. You're going back, just like that?"

Dad presses his lips in a frown. "*We're* going back, and yes. But if you feel you aren't ready now, your mother is prepared to stay in the States until the summer."

Angela utters a squeak. Her wide eyes find mine, begging me to stop this from happening. I fist my hair in my hands as options and arguments fly through my mind. It's a short list.

Dad glances away, and then Mom says, "Neither of you wanted to move here, either."

I look over to see her staring straight at me.

"You didn't want to leave your friends or your school. You hated it here at first," she reminds me, her eyes imploring me to go with this. "We hoped you would be happy to go back."

Happy? Happy to leave the first place I've ever been myself. The friends who know and like *me* for who I am, not what I can do out on the field. A girl who I realized Saturday I'm completely in love with. "Sorry to disappoint you."

Mom's face falls, but she doesn't look surprised. She knows. She gets it.

Dad is another story. "Lucas." His voice is gruff, and he coughs a few times to clear it. He shifts in his seat, clearly uncomfortable, and then wary gray eyes stare back at me. "I heard you the other day. About soccer…and…and about David." He flinches when he says my brother's name and stops to collect himself. My pulse pounds in my ears. "You may be right. I haven't taken a good look at you in quite some time. But, son, I'm looking now."

Pressure mounts behind my eyes. My throat becomes thick, and my jaw locks in place. My father searches my face as if he *is* finally seeing me. Maybe for the first time.

"If soccer isn't what you want to do, then to hell with it." My head jerks back, his words shocking the ever-loving shit out of me. "If art is your passion, then chase that. It's your life, and you have a right to spend it the way you want. David's death taught me that." Dad breaks off in a choking sound, and Mom quietly sobs.

Holy shit. Grief hits me like a truck. The pain would've brought me to my knees had I been standing. As it is, I hunch over my knees. But I don't break eye contact. Dad's clear, focused gaze is on me, and I see that he understands. Angela's hand reaches out to grasp mine.

Then he says, "But I need you to live your life in Italy."

Air whooshes from my lungs. My stomach jerks, and I sit stunned. I'm getting what I've wanted for three long years, maybe longer. Yet it's costing me everything I need.

"You can't find better inspiration than that," Mom offers softly. Always the peacekeeper. An artist who understands passion. "Milan, Florence, and Rome…Lucas, that's where my favorites lived and breathed. If you're going to follow your heart, that's the place to do it."

I shake my head, incredulous. "My heart," I repeat. "You want me to follow my heart?"

Mom's eyes widen at my tone of voice, which I admit sounds a bit crazed. But my entire fucking world has just been shoved inside a blender. "My heart lives *here*, Mom."

Her eyebrows furrow in confusion, and then awareness dawns. "You mean Cat?"

I don't answer her. I can't even if I wanted to. It's taking everything in me not to bolt or yell, or worse, give in to the burning behind my eyes. I stare back, the muscles in my jaw rippling as I strain to keep it together. Compassion washes over her face.

"I hadn't realized the two of you were that serious."

"Who is *Cat*?" Dad interrupts, glancing back and forth between us.

And that's when I lose it.

My dad's met her a half a dozen times. At her sweet sixteen months ago, here when she's come to visit, and once at her house while planning Angela's party. I've mentioned her name at countless strained family dinners. But this is how blind he's been. How utterly clueless. I've found myself because of this girl. I'm willing to fight like hell to stay here because of her. And he doesn't even know she exists.

A dark laugh explodes from my chest as I push to my feet. Dad flinches. I exchange a weighted look with Angela, and she nods, understanding my need to leave before I say or do something I'll regret. Something I can't take back and sure as shit won't help me.

Without another word, without another look at my father, I head straight for the garage, grabbing my keys off the hook as I pass the back door. As it closes behind me, I hear him call out for me, followed by Mom's gentle voice saying to give me time.

Like that will do anything.

Time isn't why I head for my bike. Riding is where I do my best thinking, and right now, I need a damn plan. A way to stay when my family up and leaves. Something I can do or say. This can't be over.

Slamming my helmet on my head, I swing my leg over the seat and check my phone before pocketing it. *One missed call.* Checking the time, I realize Cat must've called while Dad was dropping his nuclear bomb. I shove the phone deep into my pocket and turn the key.

I can't talk to her now. What would I say? *Your mom is a fake, and oh, by the way, I'm leaving you.* She's made it clear since day one her worst fear is that people leave.

My call would only confirm it.

Closure

·Cat·

I check my phone as the waiter brings me another Coke. I smile in gratitude and take a big gulp, wondering where on earth Lucas could be. After waking from my stupor yesterday (seriously, who knew partying with my *mother* could knock me on my butt so hard?), I checked my missed calls and tried calling him back. Twice. But he didn't answer.

And he hasn't called back.

What sucks is that I have this eerie feeling I can't seem to shake. A prickling on the back of my neck. A sense that someone is watching me, or something big is about to happen. I'm sure it's just this mystery with Lucas. My overactive imagination making trouble where there isn't any—that and my thrown-off sleep schedule. Nothing that copious amounts of sugar can't cure.

As I take another long pull off the sweet nectar, nearly draining the filled glass in one go, I deposit my iPhone back on the table, in clear sight in case it goes off. Although my mother is Miss Popular whose phone hasn't *stopped* ringing this morning, my screen remains black.

I frown around my straw and lift my eyes to see Ransom watching me. "Everything okay?"

Even though I'm majorly stressing, I swallow my mouthful and smile. "Yeah," I say, stabbing my drink with my striped straw. "Just being a girl. We enjoy inventing drama where there is none."

He nods as if he doesn't believe me, but he doesn't push it. After throwing Caterina an annoyed glance, he dive-bombs into his French toast. I stare at him for a minute and then go for another gulp of soda.

Ransom is another mystery I'd like to solve. Ever since he mentioned his run-in with a psychic, a dozen questions have floated in mind. Three in particular.

1. Was there anything else to the cryptic message? Can he repeat it word for word? Experience has proven that the answers to gypsy riddles are often in the fine print.

2. Did the psychic give any hint about *me*? The problem is that I haven't thought of a way to ask without appearing incredibly narcissistic. Or demented. But I'm dying to know.

3. And finally, did he manage to get her name?

Obviously, the answer to that question would only confirm what I already know is true. It was Reyna. I'm as confident about that as I am that something is up with Lucas. And while I'm trying very hard not to freak about my relationship, knowing my gypsy girl has a hand in the rest of the madness helps everything else fall into place.

This is fate. Ransom is meant to be here, and I'm meant to know my mom. The world of attention and limelight may feel like a pair of ill-fitting sneakers, but in the end, everything will work out fine. It has to. Destiny has sanctioned it.

I just need to acclimate.

After a few more minutes of quiet eating—well, Ransom and me quietly eating while Mom chatters away on her phone—she finally sets it down. Smiling at us, she asks, "Now then, where were we?"

I'm tempted to say *nowhere, since you've had your phone glued to your ear from the moment we arrived,* but I bite my tongue. Going for positivity, I say, "I have news." This gets both their attention. "Dad's wedding has been rescheduled. It's next week in Santa Barbara, and the two of you are invited."

That took no small effort on my part. They don't mind Rance, but Jenna wasn't too keen on revealing details about the big day to Caterina again. Eventually, though, they agreed that if she was going to be a part of my life, they needed to start getting along. Much to Dad's shock, the world didn't end at the premiere. They were a little twitchy about how late I was out, but in the end admitted that maybe Mom wasn't as bad as we'd once painted her to be. Maybe it was possible for people to change after all.

"Next week?" Caterina asks. Her right eye squints, and she fidgets with the silverware.

I nod, that eerie feeling pricking the base of my skull again. "Saturday."

She averts her gaze. That's not good. But before I can

work up the courage to dig, her ringtone goes off again. I don't know if I'm more ticked or relieved. She picks up her phone and squeals at the display, and I shake my head at her untouched brunch.

I've officially unearthed the secret of celebrity diets. They don't eat. Their food grows cold before they can.

"Darling!" she answers, and despite the weirdness, Ransom and I exchange a smirk. Her voice changes are majorly weird. I've heard her speak normally. I've seen glimpses of the everyday woman underneath the pancake mask. But when certain people call, or bigwigs come up to say hello, Caterina Angeli goes from girl-next-door to flirty temptress on a dime.

Nodding eagerly, Mom says, "Oh yes, I'm fully prepared. I even read through the script again last night because I love it so much. I have such a vision for this role. It's as if it was *made* for me."

That eerie feeling multiplies by a thousand as I turn and mouth to my brother, "Role?"

Ransom shrugs, clearly as clueless as I am. He leans back in his seat, dropping his fork and abandoning his plate. For a teenage guy who packs away food, that doesn't help my attack of nerves at *all*.

"How wonderful!" A smile splits Caterina's face so wide I worry it's going to crack. She snaps her fingers at the shaggy minion sitting behind us. I've recently learned his name is Brice. She pointedly lifts an eyebrow at him and asks the caller, "Tuesday?"

Brice consults his phone and nods. Caterina pumps her fist in the air. "We can do Tuesday. If you need me, I'll hop on a plane today, in fact. I'm good to go whenever production is ready." She nods again and gives Brice a thumbs-up. "How sweet. Tell Steven I look forward to working with him, too. He's absolutely brilliant."

Good grief.

As the B.S. continues to grow thicker, the knot in my gut travels north. It lodges in my chest, tightening it, making it hard to breathe. I'm not totally sure why. Mom hasn't said anything overly shady or troublesome…other than being willing to leave town at the drop of a hat. Without a second thought about Ransom or me. But she probably didn't *really* mean it, right? Just Mom being overly dramatic as always.

Still, my spidey senses are on full alert.

Grabbing what's left of my soda, I chug like there's no tomorrow.

This is what I've gathered so far.

Whoever is on the phone is important. He or she has obviously offered her a role, one that has her excited, and she thinks was made for her. I have no clue what *that* could be. It sounds as though a dude named Steven will be either her costar or the director and there's a meeting of sorts on Tuesday.

This Tuesday.

The tightness in my chest pulses. Mom promised she'd be around for a while. A few weeks she said, but at the very least, I assumed she'd be here next Saturday. I want her at Dad and Jenna's wedding. I want to see them all getting along. Having her there, looking at photographic proof later, will make this new chapter in my life feel real. Like I'll finally be able to close the door on the past, and start *fresh*.

Mom laughs. "Fantastic. I'll bring my new favorite director a box of Cubans then." She winks at Brice, and he jots it down. "Okay, sounds good. Ciao!" Caterina air-kisses the phone and disconnects.

Ransom and I lock eyes.

"Thank God mimosas have champagne!" She waves an arm to flag our waiter, and I scream at my pulse to slow the heck down.

"Good news?"

"Marvelous news," she corrects me with a full smile. Her off-camera one I've only caught glimpses of here and there. She reaches out to take both our hands and says, "I've just gotten a new lease on life. Career wise, at least," she says with a wink.

I squint in utter confusion. *Come again?*

Our young waiter appears tableside, and Caterina's smile turns flirtatious. I bite back a groan as she says, "Three mimosas and a bottle of your best champagne, hot stuff. We're celebrating."

The guy's eyebrows shoot up as she wiggles hers. He glances around our table warily. "I'm sorry, ma'am, but I'll have to see ID before I can serve everyone alcohol." Everyone of course meaning Ransom and me, the underage duo. No one's mistaking Mom for *twenty*.

I snort at the thought and quickly hide my smile behind a napkin. Then I see Caterina's frozen expression, and the napkin isn't needed. *Uh-oh.*

"Are you serious?" she asks, her voice rising at the end.

Wincing, I quickly scan the couples nearest us. As I expected, they've stopped eating, choosing instead to watch the scintillating action developing at table nine. Awesome.

The waiter adjusts his collar and nods uncomfortably. "Sorry, ma'am." Every time he says the word *ma'am*, Mom's face tightens. He transfers his weight and adds, "It's the rules. And the *law*."

Caterina's lip curls like she just sucked a lemon. "Do you even know. Who. I. *Am*?"

My jaw drops. Like, falls off and hits the table.

I've grown up hearing celebrity horror stories. Everyone has. But Dad has *never* thrown his name around. Even when I've suggested he should. Now as I watch Caterina crane her neck to see beyond our waiter, I'm really glad he's always chosen to ignore me.

"Where's your manager?" she orders.

In an instant, Sweet and Timid Waiter transforms into Mr. Feisty. His head rears back like he's prepared to do battle, and the screech of Brice's chair snags the rest of the room's attention.

This is gonna be ugly. I don't *see* any cell phones recording, but it's only a matter of time.

As Brice whispers to Caterina, I jump in to calm Mr. Feisty. Quickly pasting on a sympathetic smile, I announce to the table, "Really, it's *no* big deal. At all. I don't even like champagne."

Everyone's focus snaps to me, and our waiter takes a much-needed breath. He does not want to go toe-to-toe with Caterina Angeli.

Then Ransom says, "Me neither," and at his sharp tone, we all look to him. His guitar pick is back out, flowing across his hand like water. "I *never* drink," he says, voice like steel. "My mother is an alcoholic."

My eyes go wide, and as patrons sneak smirks at Caterina, I predict what tomorrow's headline will be. As for Mom, although her face blanches, she quickly recovers.

"I had no idea your *adoptive* mother battled such an illness. Well then," she tells our waiter with a dismissive wave of her hand. "Make that *one* mimosa and two orange juices."

I bet there will be spit in it.

Sure enough, the gleam in the waiter's eyes confirms I will not be drinking any more beverages for the remainder of our meal.

As he takes off for the kitchen, Mom turns to Ransom. "Was that necessary?"

My brother lifts an eyebrow. "I thought you wanted to get to know us, Mom. Isn't that why we're here? To bond and become a happy family," he says, repeating the publicist's words from the red carpet almost verbatim. "Motherhood is the greatest role there is, after all."

The snark is enough to give Austin a run for his money.

Caterina's heavily lined eyes flare. "Of course it is," she agrees. "But do you think airing family laundry in public is the best way to do that?"

"I've learned from the best," Ransom replies, and my hands fist under the table.

This is turning into a ping-pong match, one that I want no part in—public or otherwise.

"But that *is* why we're here," Rance pushes. "Isn't it? That's the reason you brought me to California, why you called Cat out on national television. To become a family. Right?"

His final word acts like a verbal gauntlet, and I don't blink, I don't move, as I wait to see how Caterina will react. I feel like I'm missing something, something *big,* and I'm equal parts curious and terrified. Our mother removes her napkin from her lap, dabs at a clean mouth—she hasn't eaten a thing—and twists the white linen in her hand. The longer my brother's questions hang in the air, the more I want to escape.

Caterina takes a sip of what must be lukewarm coffee, then sets down her cup. "It sounds as though you're fishing, Ransom. Is there a particular question you're trying to ask?"

Rance chuckles cynically and shakes his head. "You know, not really. This has been nothing but an experiment for me. Fodder for future lyrics." His hardened gaze swings to me and softens a fraction. "A chance to know my sister. For that, I guess I can thank you. But, no, *I* don't have any questions…"

He lifts an eyebrow, silently urging me on.

Stone-faced, I sit there, pretending I have no clue what he means. Mom, Brice, and a few nosey patrons turn their attention to me, but my focus remains on Ransom. On his strong, understanding eyes resting under stubbornly quirked eyebrows.

My chest squeezes painfully.

The thing is, I *do* know what he wants. Ransom is daring me to get my closure. To get the answers I've waited to hear for ten years. To ask the question we both know needs to be asked.

"Who was on the phone, Mom?"

Rance gives me an encouraging smile, and taking a breath, I look at Caterina. For just a second, the deer in the headlights kicks in. It's gone as quick as it comes, but it was unmistakably there, and my back teeth click. I repeat, "Who?"

Mom shrugs as if it's no big deal. "Oh, that was just Michael Layton. He's directing *It's a Quest,* a movie I've expressed interest in."

As she speaks, my mind flips back to meeting with Mr. Layton at the premiere. He knows Dad, so he went out of his way to come over and say hello...then he and Caterina went to a booth to talk with a group of men in suits. *Producers.* A burst of air expels from my lungs.

"He was calling to offer me a role," she continues with a wide smile, the kind I've gotten used to seeing on magazines, television, and the red carpet. The one that doesn't stretch her mouth or make her eyes laugh. The kind that isn't real. "I'll be playing the role of Julianne Rhodes's mother. Isn't that great?"

I nod slowly, puzzle pieces falling in place. Julianne was there the other night, too. She's your typical rising teen actress, entitled and plastered on teenybopper walls worldwide.

She's also sixteen. My age.

"Mmm-hmm." My lips are sealed shut, holding back the word vomit building inside. I inhale a long, cool breath, and as my head bobs, I realize I'm rocking in my chair.

Not because I'm sad. I'm not. I'm not scared or angry, either. Energy is zinging through my system, pulsing in my veins. Chill bumps explode on my arms. A cold sensation runs down my spine, and the rest of the restaurant fades away as I say, "And the reason he called you *now*, two days after you met with him at the premiere is..."

I purposefully trail off, wanting *her* to fill in the blanks. Curious if she'll admit the truth. The reality Ransom has obviously discovered as well.

Interestingly enough, even with a captive audience eavesdropping, Caterina doesn't disappoint. "Michael called today because the decision was just finalized," she admits, sitting back in her seat. Brice looks nauseous. "The studio has known of my interest, but they hadn't been convinced. Something about my image, and no one in America believing I'd be the right fit for the role. Can you imagine that?"

I snort, and as I shake my head and tears prick my eyes, the snort becomes a full laugh.

"*You* not motherly?" I ask, realizing and not caring that the entire restaurant is listening. Physically unable to sit still, I rub my hand along my jaw and clench a fist. "I mean, you gave your first child up for adoption when he was born, and then abandoned the second when she was only five. You never once looked back or thought about us...not until you needed something, apparently. What more could they want? That's Mother of the Year material right there!"

Brice pushes to his feet, calling out, "Check, please!" then scampers off to find help.

Ransom stares like a proud papa, and Caterina looks at me like...like...I don't even know. A week of spending time together, and my mother is still a stranger. I'd honestly thought we'd started to bond. That I was getting to see past the façade and had a chance of a real relationship with her. A shot at that sappy mother/daughter fantasy I'd always dreamed about. But I was kidding myself.

Then a thought slams into me with the force of a Mack truck. My insides squeeze, and my heart flutters.

"You know, I used to think I needed answers from you. A reason why you left. I thought I needed that to be whole. I also wondered if I was missing out, not having a mom. But see, I *do* have one. One who's good and kind. Who cares for me unconditionally, even when I treat her like crap. Who takes art lessons to understand me better and does my hair for events she doesn't want me to go to."

I shake my head as the truth washes over me. Heals me. And I notice several cell phones held up and recording my speech. I glance around with a smile, not caring.

"Jenna has been more of a mother to me in the last year than you've been in my entire life. So yeah," I say, standing up and pushing my chair in. "It is a shock that they've offered you that role. Because frankly, you as a loving mom? I don't buy it, either."

I stand there a moment, nodding my head, relishing the sensation of speaking my mind. Not caring that it'll be all over YouTube before I can even hail a cab. Owning how I feel, regardless of whether it makes a scene. Then, with a shrug of my shoulder, I grab my phone from the table and walk away.

And head toward my future.

Outside the restaurant, the noise of the city hits me in the face. I slide on my sunglasses, not to hide from the waiting paparazzi but simply because it's freaking bright out here. Ignoring the bazillion questions flying at me, I walk to the street for a cab and find Jack waiting.

The look in his eyes says he somehow already knows what I did—I guess it's his job to know.

The smile on his lips says he approves.

"In need of a ride, Miss Crawford?"

He tips his head toward the black Bronco waiting curbside, and I pat him on a bulging bicep. "Jack, my man, you read my—"

"Cat!"

Turning, I watch Rance run through the restaurant door

and promptly squint into the morning sun. I throw my hand in the air, waving it above the crowd. "Over here!"

He searches until he finds me, then shoulders his way through the maze of photographers. When he reaches me, he slumps with his hands on his knees, out of breath.

"Want a ride?" I ask, darting a questioning glance at Jack who nods. "The company will be tall and brooding, but there will be significantly less drama."

The words come out of my mouth, and they sound like me. But as Ransom straightens and watches me in concern, I realize I'm not all here. It feels like I'm floating. Talking without thinking. Standing without feeling my feet. Like an out of body experience.

My brother puts his hand on my shoulder. "You okay?"

The warmth of his hand seeps through the cotton of my shirt. My head begins to spin a little, and I quickly glance at the cameras pointed at us. "Totally," I say, pulling on my old smile — or is it a grimace? "Let's blow this Popsicle stand, huh?"

Jack tugs open the door, and Ransom helps me inside. He doesn't let go of my hand as we scoot across the bench seat, and he pulls me flush against him when we sit.

"I'm proud of you," he whispers, wrapping his arm around me. The scent of his leather jacket and maple syrup clouds my head. "That wasn't easy, but you killed it. You should've seen her face when you left."

I nod wordlessly into his chest as Jack guns the engine and peels away from the curb. Out on the road, headed for home, the full weight of what just happened catches up to me.

And I begin to cry.

Shattered

·Lucas·

The gate at the end of the drive clangs as I throw my car into park. Sealed windows muffle the clicks and hums from the paparazzi, but I can feel their stares. Jack's, too. Not caring either way, I slam my head against the seat and stare up at the roof, wishing the answers were written in the gray interior. One of Reyna's screwed-up riddles, a hint about how to begin this conversation—how not to break Cat's heart. If I'm too late, if she already caught the news or glimpsed the increased photographers staked outside her window, she probably has an idea that something's up with her mom.

But *my* news is going to blindside her.

Pain splinters through my knuckles as I ram my fist into the steering column. God, I'm an idiot. I actually fell for that mystical shit. The thought that there's more to life than what

I can see. That the world isn't just a bunch of random hits and misses, but it's somehow ordained. Planned.

If that's true, if this is *fate,* then my leaving Cat was destined from the start. I say screw that. I make my own destiny, and I'm not going anywhere.

I just have to find my loophole.

A disgusted snort escapes as I twist the keys from the ignition. *Loophole.* Right now, I'll settle for a damn thread. After riding all night and talking with Mom this morning, the best option I've got is staying here until the end of the semester. Maybe a week after.

That's three months, tops.

Fourteen weeks and then I'm supposed to just pack up and leave. Forget the person I became while I was here. The person I'm still becoming. Walk away from the people who helped me discover who that even is and the girl who makes me want more.

I might only be seventeen, but I'm a freaking expert at loss. My brother died too young. I moved halfway across the world and back for a father who has become a stranger, and I almost lost myself in the process. Friends have come and gone. A sense of security and inclusion abandoned.

And yet I found something better.

David's never coming back, but after four long years, my father just might. Soccer is finally a footnote, and my art is more focused than ever. For the first time since I can remember, I feel like I can breathe. A new future is opening up that I'm actually excited about. But Cat...Cat's my compass. She grounds me. She inspires me to be better. Her life hasn't been unicorns and rainbows, and she's still dealing with the fallout—but she hasn't given up. She puts on a good act, but she loves deep and fights harder. I need that in my life. I *want* it in my life.

I can handle everything else, but if I lose *her*, I don't know what that will do to me. And I don't intend to find out.

Exhaling with determination, I wipe my face of emotion and step from the car. Questions instantly assault me, lenses focus, but I give them nothing. My own mask is in place, aided by my new sunglasses.

Jack lifts his chin as I approach, and I shove my hands into my pockets, not wanting him or the cameras to catch a thing. Not even the anxious tremor I can't seem to shake.

When I stop in front of the door, Jack's enormous body blocks it. We've been here before, same scenario, but he knows who I am now. Is he seriously going to pat me down in front of all these cameras?

Looking up to see what his deal is, I find his attention focused straight ahead. *Okay.* I start to ask if I can go in, but shut my mouth when he clears his throat. "Busy morning."

Two words, but my mask drops in shock. Jack speaks to Cat. He obviously talks to her dad. And when necessary, he's given me monotone instructions, chin lifts, and a warning look—but he's never just shot the shit. I don't think he knows how.

From the looks of the hard smile on his face, I doubt it.

"Oh yeah?" I ask, darting a glance at the cameras.

Big guy shifts on his feet, eyes still trained on them, too. "Served a lot of clients in my time, Cappelli. Mostly jaded. The rest rude." His gaze shifts over his shoulder toward the house before sliding back to the gate. "They're different."

They meaning Cat and her family. He doesn't have to tell me that. Swallowing past the lump that's returned to my throat, I say, "I know."

Jack's jaw tenses. "Good. Because that girl of yours is something special. Been put in a shit situation she don't deserve." He looks at me then, lowering his chin so that his sunglasses shift down his nose. Dark eyes drill past my lenses. "Treat her right, yeah?"

The dude is scary as hell. Arms bigger than my head, trained to rip me apart, and I have no doubt he wouldn't hesitate to do just that. But my lips tip in a smile.

Cat says she keeps people at a distance, but she's not as tough as she thinks. The few who look past the hard shell will move mountains to protect her. Jack is one of those people. Seeing the tatted-up tough guy wrapped around her finger is added proof of just how *special* she is.

Worth fighting for.

I drop a hand on his shoulder, belatedly hoping he doesn't snap it in two. "Loving Cat is the easy part."

His lips flatten, and I take off my shades so he can see that I mean it. He scrutinizes my eyes, looking for a weakness, but I don't flinch. Loving Cat, treating her right, *is* easy. It's protecting her from the unknown that's a problem.

After a long, silent moment, he nods and falls back into position. He raps his knuckles on the front door, his face expressionless again as he says, "Glad to hear it."

· · ·

Alessandra turns and gives me a sad smile as she leads me through the foyer. That doesn't bode well. Normally, she's bubbly and can't shut up. Get her going on theater or acting, and she can talk for hours, lapsing between Italian and what

Austin calls *Shakespearean*. But when she answered the door and saw me, she didn't even mutter a hello. That *really* doesn't bode well.

When we turn down the hall, I spy Mr. Crawford in the living room. He's staring at the black screen of the television like he wants to punch it, and Jenna is crying quietly beside him. *Shit.* They must know. That's the only explanation for the tomb-like quiet and Less's selective muteness. My heart stutters and hammers as we near Cat's door…and when we walk inside, the muscle gives out completely.

I've seen Cat scared when we thought Alessandra was leaving. Cautious when Caterina first called, then hopeful at the airport. Determined just about every damn day since I met her, snarky just as often, and flirtatious on my bike. But I've never seen her broken.

My girl crying absolutely destroys me.

"Baby."

Cat sniffs as she lifts her head from Ransom's chest. From the looks of his black T-shirt, she's been using it as a tissue. Scrubbing her hands across her blotchy face, Cat looks around almost dazed until her vulnerable, gutted eyes find me. A sharp, visceral pain twists my stomach.

In three quick strides, she's out of Ransom's arms and in mine. I see the look he gives her before our eyes meet, and words aren't needed. I don't know his story, and I'm not convinced he's totally legit. But in this moment, as far as Caterina is concerned, he's got her back. With this, I can trust him.

Scooting until my back hits the headboard, I scoop her onto my lap. Cat burrows her wet face into the crook of my neck and inhales deeply. A warm puff of air hits my skin.

"You were right," she says, her voice rough from crying. "Mom sucks."

Even heartbroken, she can make me smile. "Yeah, she does." Instead of laughing or going off again when I agree, she lets out another sob, and the sound rocks through me. "God, baby, I'm sorry. So, so sorry." She clutches the cotton of my shirt, and I press my lips to her soft hair. Anger on her behalf mingles with a sense of helplessness. "Damn reporters."

She sniffs again, clearly trying to regain control, and rolls her head onto my shoulder. Her swollen eyelids blink open and her voice cracks as she asks, "What reporters?"

I smooth her hair away and kiss her forehead. I can't stop touching her. It's the only thing I *can* do. I can't erase her mom from coming here. I can't rewrite history and give her a mother who isn't a monster. But I can hold her until the pain of it goes away.

"The ones who got you so upset." Just saying it sends a fresh batch of rage surging through me. "This crap isn't newsworthy, but does that matter? The world *needs* to know about stupid movie roles," I say sarcastically, "and vapid celebrity opinions on your family." My jaw aches as I fight back the anger. "It's all such bullshit."

The splotchy skin between Cat's eyebrows wrinkles. "Wait, what are you talking about?" Shoving the heels of her hands into her eye sockets, she rubs away the moisture and scoots higher in my lap. "Luc, this literally just happened. I got home from brunch with my lying POS mom not twenty minutes ago. Were you stalking YouTube or something?"

Brunch?

Ransom shoots me a glance, but I'm too confused to read

it. I guess there is more to Cat's meltdown than I thought. Instantly, I imagine the worst. The director showing up and interrupting their meal. The actress who will be playing her daughter. Caterina leaving without her. Again.

"What's on YouTube?"

The way she stiffens tells me that wasn't the right response. Suspicion washes over her face before she pushes against my chest. I help her sit up, waiting until she is cross-legged in front of me before locking my arms around her lower back. I know she's trying to pull away from me. I can feel it. But it's not the physical distance that scares me.

"If you don't know about it, then why are you here?" Her throat tenses as she swallows, and then her face clears. A piece of her armor falling into place. "The first thing you said when you walked in was 'I'm sorry.' You apologized for something that's not even your fault, and then you cursed reporters." The same wall that took me a month to topple builds with each word, blocking the pain. Keeping me out. By the time she stops to take a long breath, the mask is completely back. "So again, Luc, I gotta ask. What. *Reporters*?"

The calm, collected girl with red-rimmed eyes is not *my* Cat. It's the public Cat, the one the world knows. Photographers, journalists, even our classmates. But I haven't seen this girl since the night of her birthday party.

My pulse picks up again as fear spikes. I'm already fighting my parents and Reyna's damn stars for a way to stay with her. I refuse to let Cat be the one to push me away. Not over this.

So while this is not how I planned to tell her, I go with the truth. "Yesterday I caught a segment on an entertainment channel. About your mom and some movie role."

"Yesterday," Cat repeats, blinking her matted lashes slowly. She scrunches her mouth and jabs an elbow into the barrier of my arms, forcing me to let go, then knocks my hands away as she scoots back a foot. "Was that before or *after* I called you?"

A look of betrayal slips through her mask, and I realize my mistake.

But before I can answer or explain, she shakes her head. "You know what, it doesn't matter. You kept it from me. I've been a nervous wreck, Luc. I didn't know why, it didn't make sense. *One day* you didn't call me back. Big deal. I told myself you were busy with Angela, or maybe the thing with your dad came to a head." She huffs a laugh, but not the happy one she let loose on my bike. "But I had a *feeling* something was wrong."

The way she says it, I know what she means. She's talking about that hocus-pocus crap again. The thing I almost believed—and if it *is* real, the thing trying to rip us apart. Frustration has me tearing at my hair.

"A feeling, huh? What, did Reyna whisper that in your ear? Chant on the wind? Ever occur to you that maybe life's a little more serious than magic and feelings?"

"Seriously?" Her voice is hard as stone as she pushes to her knees on the mattress. "You mean like finding out my mother's been playing me this whole time? Cell phones capturing my whole freaking meltdown? And then discovering my boyfriend *knew* and didn't warn me?"

Shit. My eyes widen as I realize what just went down. "Whoa." I hold my hands up, knowing I need to scale things back. "I don't even know why I said that. I didn't mean it. I know I should've said something. That's why I'm here now. To tell you what I saw. I swear, baby, if I knew you were meeting her this morning—"

"If you'd called me back, you would have."

I swallow hard, trying to regain control of the situation. I glance away and see Alessandra still standing at the door, wide-eyed and frozen, and Ransom inching closer to the exit. "Right," I say. "You're right. If I had called or texted you, I would've known about brunch. But something came up with my dad, and I just needed to get out and clear my head."

The moment I say it, I realize my second mistake. Cat's eyes grow sharp as she asks, "What came up?"

The tremor is back in my hands. I lock them behind my head as beads of sweat prick my skin. This is the worst possible time to dump this on her. We're fighting over something stupid, and she's already emotional. If I don't play this right, it could go from bad to apocalyptic in an instant.

But she's already pissed at me for keeping quiet. I can't *not* tell her.

"I really don't think this is the right—"

"Spit it out, Luc."

Her voice is cold as steel, and I drop my chin to my chest. "My parents are moving back to Milan."

The whoosh of air I feel is Cat jumping off the bed.

Lifting my head to stare into her wide brown eyes, I say, "Did you hear what I said? I said my *parents* are moving back, Cat. Not me. I'm not going anywhere."

Her mask slips again, and I see the hurt, fear, and anger. Her go-to response is always to push people away, to keep this very thing from happening. I know that's what she wants to do now. Moving to the edge of the bed, I plant my feet. "I made you a promise that I wasn't like the others. That I wasn't going anywhere. I keep my promises, Cat."

She says nothing as her jaw locks, the muscles in her throat working.

A formal, softly spoken question breaks the silence. "They will let you stay?"

It comes from Alessandra, but my gaze never leaves Cat's face. "I'm still working on that part," I admit. She wraps her arms around her chest like she's holding the pain in, and I wish those were my arms around her. "I haven't figured it out yet, but I *will*," I say, begging her with my eyes to believe me. "I'm not giving up. I'll do whatever I have to do."

The hardwood floor creaks as Ransom shifts his feet and glances at Alessandra. "We'll give you two a minute."

I nod, silently thanking him.

But he only manages a step before Cat says, "No, stay."

Ransom drops his head. Alessandra bites her lip like she's trapped, but I'm more worried about the determination solidifying on my girlfriend's face. When Cat's eyes meet mine, I know it's going to be bad.

"Save yourself the trouble."

Pain explodes in my chest, even as I doubt my hearing. She didn't just say that.

Ransom sighs and says, "Cat…" but trails off at the sharp look she throws him. He shakes his head but stays quiet, sending me a sympathetic smile.

I don't want sympathy. I want Cat. I want the life that I've been building here, the friends, the future. I want my girl to fight for me as hard as I'm fighting for her. Not throw in the damn towel the second trouble hits.

Hurt and anger boil under my skin, and I look away, glaring when my gaze lands on the painting Ransom is leaned against. I can't read the plaque from here, but I know what it says. GODDESS VICTORIA WITH PAINTED PEAR, LORENZO CAPPELLI, 1506.

Maybe I'm an idiot for wanting to stay. To fight for this. Maybe I am just a stand-in for her first love after all. But when I turn back to Cat, I look at her. *Really* look at her. I note the tracks of tears on her face, the lost look in her eyes…and I know she's hurting. Hurt over her mom and hurt because she thinks I'm leaving. Lashing out is what she does best.

So I say, "You can push me away all you want, little badass, but I'm not Caterina. I'm not those stupid friends who bolted when you were a kid. I'm not the paparazzi, I'm not a reporter, and I'm sure as hell not someone looking at you expecting anything other than what you are. Cat Crawford, kickass artist." I stand up and take a step toward her. "The girl I love."

Her soft lips part as Alessandra squeaks behind us. I've never said the words before. I've hinted, I've showed, but never came right out and declared it. But if ever there was a time to put all my cards on the table, this is it.

I let the words settle in the air, and then I say, "I'll give you some time, if that's what you want. Some space if that's what you need to figure out how you feel. What it is you want. But I already know what *I* want."

Cat's gaze is on my mouth, as if she can see the words as they leave. "You do?"

I fight back a smile and nod. It's been a long time since I could say what I wanted was crystal clear—but it is. "And I don't give up easily."

Space Blows

·Lucas·

The bell rings, and I chuck my pencil on my desk. Sizing up my sketch, I immediately see all the flaws. Most days I'm a decent artist, but with Cat sitting only one row away, not-so-subtly watching me from behind a curtain of thick hair, it's impossible to even draw a straight line. I can feel her eyes on me. It's hard as hell not to look back, but I don't. I *want* her to watch.

Watching means that she misses me, too.

It's been six days since our fight in her room. Almost an entire week. And in that time, I've come to the conclusion that doing the right thing blows. When I left her house Saturday, I said I'd give her space to think. As much as she needed to be as sure about us as I am. At the time, I even meant it. Now, not so much.

I miss Cat. I miss hearing her sarcastic jabs, seeing the love that I know was building for me shining in her eyes. I miss talking to her, getting her opinion. She's smart as hell. Quick, too. If she were helping me find this damn loophole, it'd be found already. But like I told her before I walked away, I keep my promises. If she needs space to realize that we're meant to be together, and that nothing—not fate *or* my parents—is going to stop that, then space is what she'll get.

Doesn't keep it from blowing, though.

"Mr. Cappelli, can I speak with you for a minute?"

In my peripheral, I see Cat glance over as I nod. "Sure thing, Mr. Scott."

It's weird when most teachers call us by our last names, like they're pretending we're somehow equals. With Mr. Scott, I don't really mind. The man's got mad talent, and I respect the hell out of him. I know that goes both ways.

I pack up my stuff, fighting a smirk when I see Cat taking her sweet time doing the same. As I walk up the aisle, I feel her gaze follow every step. When I know she can no longer see my face, I smile. "What's up?"

"Hopefully a bit of good news." Reaching into his leather satchel, Mr. Scott pulls out a stack of papers. "This was waiting in my box this morning, along with a message from Mr. Allen."

He hands over the papers, and relief centers in my chest at the name written on top. Trying and failing to keep the hope out of my voice, I ask, "I'm in?"

"Well, I guess that's up to your folks." Mr. Scott's eyes are proud as he adds, "But the committee was impressed, like I knew they would be. Now it comes down to your negotiation skills."

And my father's stubbornness.

That knocks the smile right off my face. This is only one cleared hurdle — I still have the biggest yet to come. But I don't want to seem ungrateful. Mr. Scott went to bat for me, hard. "Thank you for doing this," I tell him, knowing the words aren't nearly enough. "I really appreciate it."

He claps a hand on my shoulder. "My pleasure, son. I mean that. You have talent, and I expect great things from you. Selfishly, I'd like to be close enough to see them."

He smiles as he jostles my arm, and I crack a half smile. "When I have my first solo exhibition, your name will be at the top of the list," I promise. "And when I win the Skowhegan Medal for Sculpture, you'll be the first person I thank."

Might as well dream big, right?

Mr. Scott laughs and slaps me on the back. "I'm holding you to that."

I follow him out the door and into the hall, listening for Cat's footsteps behind me. Mr. Scott asks me to come see him in the morning, hopefully with good news, and I watch as he heads to the teacher's lounge. I slow my stride as I near Cat's next class.

"Hey, Luc?"

My chest squeezes at the sound of my name on her lips. Almost a week ago, I told her I loved her. She didn't say the same. It'd be a lie to say that doesn't hurt. I turn around and back against the lockers, away from the frantic crowd. "Yeah?"

Cat glances at the ground. Hiking the strap of her schoolbag higher on her shoulder, she bites her lip and then asks, "Is everything okay? With Mr. Scott, I mean? I heard the two of you talking."

A flush sweeps her cheeks as she realizes she admitted to stalking me. It's so tempting to pull her into my arms and kiss away the stain, to tell her everything. About what I've found out, the steps I've taken…prove that I'm keeping my promise and that I'm not going anywhere.

But what if this doesn't work? Dad still has to agree—and that's a major question mark. I can't get her hopes up until I know for sure. Plus, other than the stalking, she hasn't given me any sign that she wants me to hold her. That's she's ready to fight for us.

"Yeah, everything's good," I say instead, shoving the papers from SFBSA in my notebook. "Mr. Scott's just helping me with something."

"Oh." Cat rocks back on her heels, still working her bottom lip between her teeth. I know firsthand how soft that lip is…how warm. Swallowing, I force my eyes back to hers. She blinks, and for a moment, the curtain falls. I see the vulnerability and sadness. "I hope whatever it is works out," she says vaguely. She slides her hand along the strap of her backpack, pausing to mess with a dangling thread. The distance between us feels so much bigger than a floor tile. She exhales and takes a step closer. "Listen, I—"

A second chime erupts overhead, the signal that our next class is starting.

"Never mind." She shakes her head and forces a smile. "It can wait."

I inwardly curse the bell. Whatever she was about to say, I want to hear it. I crave it. It's been 144 hours of silence, interrupted by stolen looks and longing. The idea that she's as miserable as I am is like a sick need inside me. I don't want her hurt… I just want her back.

The hallway empties, and she glances at the door behind me. She only has to step inside. My next class is across campus, which means I'll be hoofing it. But it's been worth it. This brief connection, as pathetic as it may seem, is enough to fuel me for what lies ahead.

"Guess I better get to bio," she says, her eyes locked back on mine. I nod as she slowly walks forward, watching her hesitant progress until she disappears through the classroom door. Then I yank out the papers that could determine my future.

• • •

"Lucas?"

Mom frowns as she pushes to her feet across from Dad's desk. As for my old man, he leans back in his chair, eyes sharp on my face. Clearly, they're surprised to see me home so early. They should be — I bailed on my last class.

I swear I held out for as long as I could. Those papers wore a damn hole in my notebook as I sat through class after class, not able to concentrate on a freaking thing. I just sat there rehearsing my speech in my head. Finally, as the bell rang for French, I'd had enough. I realize skipping won't do me any favors in proving I'm ready to handle major life decisions. It very well may bite me in the ass before I even begin. But this conversation couldn't wait any longer. I have my plan, the boxes are checked, and I'd really rather have it all go down without Angela around. I don't want her caught in the middle if it gets ugly.

Dad closes the ledger on his desk. He taps a rhythm on the leather surface with his pen, emotions flashing across his face. More than I've seen in years. Curiosity followed by annoyance. Guilt trailed by regret. What I don't see is resignation, which I choose to take as a good sign. I grab a seat across from him as Mom returns to hers, and the three of us sit in heavy silence. Dad waits me out, gaze focused and heavy, but I can't rush this. My future relies on everything going absolutely right.

After what feels like forever, could be a minute, Mom speaks up. "You have something you need to talk with us about?"

I almost laugh. I should've expected she'd be the one to cave first. Always the peacekeeper. In answer to her question, I reach into my bag and pull out the papers from Mr. Scott. I place them on Dad's desk, and he lifts an eyebrow as he scans the cover page. "I have an alternative to Milan."

Dad's shaking his head before the words are even out of my mouth. "Absolutely not."

"An alternative?" Mom hesitantly scoots forward in her chair and cranes her neck to read the papers. "What is SFBSA?"

"San Francisco Bay School for the Arts," I tell her, watching the tick of my father's jaw. "It's a boarding school a few hours away, and it's one of the top five programs like it in the world. A degree from here will get me into any college I want."

Dad scoffs. "And your sudden interest has nothing to do with a certain girl?"

The question, or rather the way he asks it, pisses me off...but he's right. At least partially. If it weren't for Cat,

I more than likely would've never even heard of SFBSA. I certainly wouldn't have gone to Mr. Scott and asked about local boarding school options. But it's not just about Cat anymore. It's about *me*, and that's what I need both of them to see.

"No," I say, meeting and holding his gaze. "You're right. Cat is the reason why I looked into this place at first. But she's not why I want to go…or at least, she's not the only reason. She's not even the most important."

That seems to catch their attention. Dad's eyebrows hike farther up his forehead as he leans forward in his chair and rests his folded arms on the desk. Mom places a gentle hand on my arm. With those two subtle hints for me to continue, I go on and lay it all out there.

"You were right the other day about Italy. It *is* an amazing place to study art. I know. I was there. And going back to do that will always be an option. During the summer, on holidays, maybe even for college. But not right now. Now, I want to stay *here*. On my own."

The words fall like a bomb, and I let them sink in for a moment.

Then I say, "Look, I've spent the past four years not even knowing who I am or what I want." Swallowing past a strange lump in my throat, I say, "I need to find that out."

Mom squeezes my arm. I look over to see tears welling in her eyes. "But, Lucas, you don't have to be alone to do that. Your father and I know we've made mistakes, but we're here for you. We hope you know that."

Closing my hand over hers, I nod. "I know that. And I swear, this isn't about me blaming you. I did this to myself. Since David died, I've been every bit as lost and hurt as the two of you. But if I want to be a man"—I turn and look my father in the eyes—"the kind of man you've raised me to be, then I need to figure this out on my own. I feel like it's the only way I can get the answers I need."

Dad's narrowed eyes soften. With pride or pity, I don't know, but I decide to go forward with my speech anyway.

"I need to find direction...in art *and* in life. I want to stand on my own two feet and surround myself with the world's best artists. Who knows, maybe I'll decide that art should just be a hobby. Maybe I'll go on to business school like you wanted." I'm pretty sure I get him with that one. "Or maybe I'll see that I do have what it takes after all," I add before he gets too excited. "Either way, I'll have tested myself. Alone, with no more excuses. Starting fresh, I'll figure it out. I know it."

It's true, too. Call it whatever you want, but there's a rock of certainty in my gut, telling me this is the right thing to do. It started as a knot when I first heard about the place. Now that I know it's an actual possibility, it's a solid mass. With or without Cat by my side, I need this. But it will be so much better if she's with me.

My father exchanges a long look with my mother and releases a heavy breath. "Lucas, what you're saying is admirable. I respect it, and I'm damn proud of the young man sitting in front of me. But, son, you're seventeen years old. I can't just leave you in another country."

I expected as much, which means—thankfully—I have an answer. "I'll be a senior next year." I glance at Mom, including her as I say, "That's one year away from leaving for college. You always said I could go anywhere I wanted then... What's twelve months? If it doesn't work out, I can come home, and you can say 'I told you so.' But this chance fell into my lap, and it feels like what I'm supposed to do."

Mom cracks first, turning to Dad with what looks to be curiosity and maybe even a hint of petition in her eyes.

Hope surges through me, almost making me light-headed as I rush to add, "They've already accepted me. Mr. Scott sent them samples of my work and a copy of my transcript." I glance back and forth between them, wishing I were a mind reader. "All they need, all *I* need, is your permission."

The silence that follows is weighted. It's long and sends pricks of apprehension down my back. As they do their wordless parent communication thing, it feels like everything waits in the balance. If this doesn't work, I won't give up. I promised Cat I wouldn't. If it means I have to keep searching or if I have to hop on a plane every month to see her, I'll do it. But I meant what I told my parents. This school, this decision, is bigger than my love life. It's my *whole* life.

Dad scrubs a hand across his face. His voice sounds changed, almost weary, when he asks, "This is something you really want?"

I take a breath and say honestly, "It's something I really need."

He nods once and glances briefly at my mother again. "Then let's talk."

My Stupid Mouth

·Cat·

Seriously, sometimes I need a muzzle. Like the one that mean chick put on Lady in *Lady and the Tramp*. Without it, I spew things I don't mean. Or I say things I *think* I mean in the heat of the moment, but end up regretting forever.

Case in point? My verbal vomit disaster in my room with Lucas. Today's awkward encounter in the hall was the first time we've spoken in almost a week. He's stayed away, giving me space like he said he would—like I all but forced him to give—because that's what I *said* I wanted. Honestly, the only thing I've wanted since the door closed behind his perfect backside, and Alessandra gave me those puppy dog eyes, is to rewind time and start over.

Less keeps hounding me to tell him I'm sorry, that I was angry with my mom and scared about him leaving, and I lashed out.

But what if it's too late?

That's what keeps me frozen, resorting to eyeball stalking him in the halls and the one measly class we share. What if my freak-out has given Lucas the chance to step back and realize that he's better off without me after all? That I have *way* too much baggage and am too high maintenance?

I look down and close my hand around my eight-petal charm as memories assault me. The day he gave this to me, Valentine's Day, was easily one of the happiest of my life. I'd never felt that close to anyone. More wanted, more in love. Because that's what I know without a doubt that I am—in *love*. The same thing Lucas claimed to be before I tossed him out on his gorgeous rear.

Shaking my head, I stare at my idiot reflection in the lavish hotel mirror. The thick makeup covering the circles under my eyes. The bright lipstick coating my mouth, attempting to compensate for my sallow complexion. Outside this bathroom, people are laughing and eating. Toasting Dad and Jenna at their rehearsal dinner. As for the happy couple, they're totally blissed out—as well they should be. Lord knows *they've* dealt with my stupid mouth enough over the years. They deserve to celebrate their relationship surviving me.

Now if only *mine* can do the same.

"Knock, knock."

I glance up to see Alessandra peek her head around the thick door and give me a timid smile.

"Are you all right, dear cousin?" she asks, gently closing the door and leaning her back against it. "You have been gone for quite some time."

"Peachy," I reply sarcastically, sighing and tossing my head back. The ceiling is painted a light cream, with gold wispy things and pink roses along the edges. *Roses.* I sigh again and lower my chin. "I'm happy for Dad. Really. Jenna is the best thing that's ever happened to him, and I'm so glad to see him in love with a woman who really appreciates him, you know?"

Unlike my selfish mother, who obviously doesn't know the meaning of love.

Less glides toward the plush sofa against the wall and pats the open space next to her. "I do know," she says. "Although I have only lived with you for a short time, I can see how Jenna fits him. She comes alongside him and takes care of him, supports him, inspires him to be better. Much like he does for her." She smiles as she takes my hand, turning slightly on the cushion to face me. "And like Lucas does for you."

"Dang, girl. Hit a chica when she's down, why don't you?"

The true extent of how well Less has fit into my world is proven when she simply shrugs a shoulder and gives me a *you-asked-for-it* look.

I can't help but laugh a little as I say, "But since you so *kindly* brought it up, yeah, like that. Actually, exactly that. And it's just hard being out there when they are so happy. I'm truly, honestly, one hundred percent stoked for them, but smiling and pretending that I'm happy, too? I used to rock that business, but I just can't do it anymore. I've officially lost my mojo." I glance at the door, imagining I can see my smiling Dad beyond the wood. "And I don't want to bring them down with my mopeyness."

She shakes her head like I'm a moron, which, let's face it, considering my actions of late, isn't that far off the mark. "Cat, he's your *father*." I don't miss the way her voice catches ever so slightly, no doubt thinking of her own father, Uncle Marco, back in the sixteenth century. "He *wants* to be there for you." She pins me in place with the solemn look in her eyes. "Just as the rest of us do."

My chest grows tight under the intensity of her stare. I know what she's getting at. What everyone is getting at. Less, Lucas, Dad…Reyna, they all want the same thing. To care for me.

"I'm scared," I whisper.

Alessandra wraps her arm around my shoulders and sets her head against mine. "I know you are," she says and kisses my temple. "But this is part of your journey. The same one you started months ago." The words sound so much like something Reyna would say that I lift my head to look at her. She smiles gently, like she knows what I'm thinking, and says, "It's time."

Chills rush down my spine. She's right. I know she is. But can I do it?

The door opens again, and this time my brother's head materializes. "Interrupting girl bonding time?"

I shake my head, and he tromps inside, seemingly not at all weirded out that this is the *women's* bathroom. He plops down on the sofa and winks.

Gender issues aside, I'm glad he's here. Our relationship is new, and we have a lot left to learn, but he's family. Every bit as much as Alessandra is. Maybe it's because he looks so much like my cousin. Maybe it's that sibling bond thing. Maybe it's because this is fate, and we were supposed to be in each other's lives—but this feels right.

My mother hurt me. Caterina used me for her own gain and fooled me in a lot of ways. But I got my closure. In the end, she actually gave me something better than that.

She gave me a brother.

Sandwiched between my cousin from a different time and the sibling I never knew existed, I feel strangely at peace. Almost everyone I care about is in this hotel or is driving up tomorrow. There's only one thing keeping the wedding from being perfect.

"Nah," I say with a shake of my head. "Not girl bonding time. More like 'Berate Cat for Being an Idiot' time."

Ransom nods slowly, then glances at Alessandra over my head. "This about the lovesick boyfriend?"

Less lifts her eyebrows, and I snort. "Excuse me, but shouldn't the two of you be rushing to defend my genius? Consoling me. Making me feel better. Isn't that what family…a-and friends," I quickly add when Less widens her eyes, "do?"

Both of them just stare at me blankly, neither making a peep, and I blow out a breath.

Well, then.

"Oh, what the hell am I talking about?" I ask, slumping back against the luxurious velvet couch. "I *am* an idiot. I pushed away *my* Jenna, the best thing that's ever happened to *me*. But then, that's what I do. I protect myself. I hurt them before they can hurt me. Rah-rah sis boom ba. I am woman, hear me roar." I chuckle darkly up at the roses mocking me from the ceiling. "If there was a black belt in severe idiocy, I'd own that sucker."

Rance chuckles as he shifts beside me. "This a pattern of

yours, I take it?"

I loll my head to meet his concerned gaze. "Pretty much. At least since dear old mom took off. It's my defense from the hurt of being left behind. If no one gets close enough to care about, it can't sting when they decide to bolt."

Tucking a strand of hair behind my ear, Rance says softly, "Not everyone leaves."

The deep breath I take stutters in my chest. "You plan on sticking around then?"

I'm sure he's going to say no. That he's going to sit there and prove my theory. He has a life in Houston. Friends. Why would he bother staying here? So when his smile turns almost shy, and he lifts his shoulder in a shrug, my jaw drops. "I've been thinking about it."

Alessandra gets up and daintily kneels on the carpet in front of me. "See, Cat? This is what I mean. You have to stop pushing away the people who love you," she tells me. "We are not all like your mother. Your father, Jenna, Austin and me, your brother, and Lucas…we love you."

Her words hit me full in the chest, and I wince. Hot tears prick my eyes. I close them and bow my head.

I know they love me. I love them, too. That's what makes this so stinking hard. The pain I'm feeling isn't anyone else's fault but my own. Lucas didn't leave me—at least not yet. The loneliness, the fear, the hurt…I'm doing it all to myself. And I'm hurting Lucas, too.

Who knew pushing someone away—someone who truly matters—could cut deeper than being abandoned?

Less places her hands on my knees and ducks down to meet my gaze. "None of us are going anywhere. Even if Lucas does end up leaving, it is not the end of the world.

Not with the wonderful, modern conveniences of today."
She grins as she says this, and I look over to see Ransom
quirk an eyebrow. If he plans to hang around, we probably
need to fill him in on a few things soon. I smile despite my
leaking eyes and turn back when Alessandra squeezes my
knee. "Please…trust us enough to let us in."

A clean white handkerchief appears in front of my
eyes, and I accept it from my brother. Why a nineteen-year-
old dude even owns a handkerchief is beyond me, but I'm
grateful. Picture time is coming any minute. The last thing
I need is eternal, smudgy-faced proof that I'm an idiot.
Dabbing carefully under my eyes, I sniff and ask, "Since
when did you become the Miyagi of this relationship?"

Even though the *Karate Kid* reference flies over her
head, she grins and replies, "Well, you should always listen
to your elders."

"Okay, what?"

At Rance's look of utter confusion, we bust out laughing.

When I visited the sixteenth century, Alessandra was
two years younger than me. When she appeared here
two months later, she'd somehow magically caught up.
Technically, however, the girl is *five hundred* years my senior.

I guess she gets a few wisdom points for that.

We're still giggling, and Rance is still confused, a few
moments later when the door opens again. Jenna peeks
her head inside, looking bridal and beautiful in a long
white cocktail dress, signature megawatt smile on her face.
"Picture time!"

My old-school, handkerchief-wielding brother is the first
to his feet. He gallantly takes our hands, assisting us up, and
I sneak a stealth glance in the mirror. Everything appears in

order. No mascara tracks or raccoon eyes. Unfortunately, my future stepmother must have some kind of radar because as we approach, Jenna's beaming smile dims.

"Everything all right?" she asks, clasping a manicured hand around my elbow.

"Everything's fine." I signal for Alessandra and Ransom to go on ahead.

Less gives a thumbs up behind Jenna's shoulder, then follows her brother's doppelganger down the hall.

Turning back to Jenna, I smile like a dope and go for humor, singsonging the words I so badly want to say. The words I know she needs to hear. "Have I told you lately that I love you?"

The obvious answer would be *no,* since I've never said those words to her *ever.* But I know that doesn't matter. What's important is that I'm saying it now. And that I mean it. Jenna's big blue eyes fill with tears at my crappy singing, and I hand over Rance's handkerchief.

"Because I do," I tell her sincerely, dropping the smile. "I have for a long time, I've just been too scared to admit it. To you or myself. But I want you to know before you walk down that aisle tomorrow that I'm grateful you came into our lives. You make Dad happier than I've ever seen him."

Those silent tears of hers turn into blubbery sounds as she smashes the cloth against her face. But the blue eyes peeping over the top look happy—no, they look *accepting.* Loving. Joyous.

Swallowing past the thickness in my throat, I add, "You make *me* happy, too."

The next thing I know, slender arms are yanking me in for a tight hug, and I'm enveloped in her light, fruity perfume. Four months ago, I loathed these kinds of sappy things. I avoided them at all costs. Now? It's kind of nice.

In moderation.

I hug her back, the scent of strawberry filling my nose as I say, "You're a wonderful person, Jenna. It'll be an honor to officially call you Mom."

She shakes her head and leans back, laughing softly. "Cat, you've been the daughter of my heart for a year now." Running a hand over my hair, a sweet, watery smile slides across her face. "And believe me, the honor is all mine."

A Kick in the Ass

·Lucas·

"I'll never see a California summer." Angela falls onto my mattress, a dramatic sigh escaping her turned-up mouth. "Send me a postcard of it, will you?"

She bats her eyelashes, and I slap my chest, feigning chest pains. "Teasing hurts, you know."

After Dad agreed to talk with the school and Mr. Scott, I was cautiously optimistic. When he and Mom came to my room last night, saying they'd decided to give boarding school a shot—on a trial basis—I was relieved. But I wasn't happy. Not only was my relationship with Cat still up in the air, I had to tell my sister the news. She'd begged me to find a way for *both* of us to stay, and the solution I found was a selfish one.

"Oh, lighten up," she says, rolling her eyes. "Will you just call the girl already? You're zero fun when you're all serious. And you know I'm just messing with you."

While I spent the last week plotting and planning for a way to stay, my sister apparently spent the time calling old friends in Milan. Turns out, she doesn't much mind moving again, as long as she can finish out the year here and have her huge party. Her former crush getting wind of her plans and calling the other night didn't hurt, either.

"You're seriously okay with this?" I ask her again, just to be sure. I set aside the clay I was kneading for a new sculpture and wipe my hands on a rag. "You know you can visit me any time you want."

She nods and sits up. "I'm good. I did tell Dad that if they make me move again, he owes me a Ferrari," she says with a grin, and I have no doubt she did. Even when he was checked out of our family, Angela had the old man practically wrapped around her finger.

I chuckle at the thought of her behind the wheel, even as the vision of another Ferrari comes to mind.

"Speaking of cars," Angela says, hopping off the bed, "you have a customer."

Lifting an eyebrow, I ask, "Huh?"

"A visitor," she says, that mischievous smile back on her face again. This time it totally confuses me. "Austin Michaels wants you to tune up his engine."

Forget confusion. I'm dumbfounded. Sure, I love being under the hood, and Austin knows it. But since when does he need a handout? With the money his dad throws around, and his outstanding taste in cars, I wouldn't be surprised to find out they've got a live-in mechanic.

And shouldn't Austin be in Santa Barbara?

I follow my sister out to the living room where Austin is sprawled on my couch. "What's up, man?" I hit his fist as he sits up. "Shouldn't you be with Less at the wedding?"

"Heading there next," he says, glancing at his clothes.

I hadn't paid attention before but now I can see his usual thrown-together look is tamer. His hair even has gel in it. I hold back the urge to screw with him and ask, "Then why the hell are you here?"

Not that I'm not grateful for the distraction. Since I woke up, it's been an ongoing mission to keep myself from bolting out the door and seeing Cat in that sexy dress that's been hanging in her closet. She rarely wears dresses, and that glimpse on TV from the premiere was tainted.

"Angela said something is up with your truck?"

Austin smirks and slides his keys out of his pocket. "Not exactly." He exchanges a weird look with my sister and then heads toward the foyer. Great, now they have Austin speaking Reyna-cryptic.

Shaking my head, I walk out the front door. It takes a second for me to understand what I'm seeing. When I do, my jaw drops and I curse. "No way." I backpedal to my door, palms up. "No way in hell. I'd give anything to see what's under her hood, but your dad will literally kill me if I mess anything up."

Austin laughs and slaps me on the shoulder. "Dude, I'm not here for your professional services. I'm here to give you a kick in the ass."

I look away from the Ferrari Enzo and see Austin holding out the keys. He drops them in my opened hand, and my fingers close around the cool metal. "What the hell?"

"Incentive," he explains. "You're so worried about doing

the right thing. Being noble and shit, doing what you think Cat wants. Man, I love the girl like she's a sister, but since when has knowing what she wants and saying it been her strong suit?"

I can't help but laugh at that. It's the damn truth. But in this case, I wanted her to come to *me*. I already put everything on the line for her. She knows how *I* feel.

I want her to want me as much as I want her.

"Less is chirping in my ear, worried about her cousin and wanting to play Cupid. Cat dragged ass all week and moped the entire rehearsal." Austin looks me up and down and pulls a face. "And I hate to tell you, man, but you look like crap. What are you waiting for?"

A stupid thrill runs through me, knowing she's miserable. How twisted is that? As for what I'm waiting for, I thought it was for her to fight for us. To woman up and come after *me*.

But Austin's right. That's not Cat. In everything else, that girl is hard as nails. But when it comes to her heart, she's totally vulnerable. This is new for her. Hell, just being with me is a freaking miracle, not to mention a monumental step. And here I am pushing for it all after only a couple months.

I guess the better question is not "what am I waiting for." It's do I want to be *happy*, and be with Cat?

Or do I just want to be right?

I inhale deeply and nod, knowing what I have to. What I should've done a long time ago.

Austin's face lights up, and he smacks me on the back. "That's what I'm talking about," he calls out, shoving me toward the driver's door. "Stop being noble and start being the damn hero."

He waits until I pop open the door before he slides into

the passenger seat. I put the key in the ignition and listen to the baby purr. The thrum of the engine feeds into me, and my heart starts pounding. The drive to Santa Barbara is ninety minutes. The wedding starts in just over that. I give my casual jeans and shirt a glance. There's no time to change, but what I'm wearing doesn't matter. The only thing that does is getting Cat back.

I buckle up, ready to break one promise to keep another—the first one I ever gave her. I smile, remembering the night we finally got together.

"Cat, the night I met you," I told her, "everything clicked into place for me. The move to the States was suddenly a blessing instead of a curse, and life made sense again. I won't pretend to understand why you're so determined to fight the feelings I know you have for me, too, but I just wanted you to know that I'm here." I took a step forward. "I'm not going anywhere." I took another step and brushed a strand of hair away from her face. "I felt something between us the night of your party, and I feel it between us now, and I'm not gonna give up. Not until you tell me to."

Now, with a glance in the rearview mirror, I say, "Let's go get my girl."

Grand Gestures

·Cat·

Getting made-over by Jenna's team is strangely reminiscent of my stay in the sixteenth century. Only instead of Lucia—the young servant girl who pampered me then—I have a team of professionals styling my hair, doing my makeup, and primping my nails. With Jenna on one side and Less on the other, this would be relaxing and total girl-time bonding bliss…if my mind weren't completely preoccupied with thoughts of Lucas.

All is right in the world of Jenna and me. The same goes for my relationship with Ransom. Dad is happy, Alessandra is good, and my birth mother is back where she belongs—out of my life. The small hotel we rented for the wedding today is swarming with friends and family, and almost everyone I care about is within the building. Everyone but Lucas.

my not so *Super Sweet* life

"I'd offer this for your thoughts," Jenna says, her glamorous reflection holding up a bright, shiny penny. "But something tells me I don't need it."

Alessandra makes a noise of agreement as Jenna slides the *lucky* coin back into her shoe, her reflected sad eyes never leaving mine. This is so wrong. Her eyes should be glistening with tears of love and joy, not sympathy over my relationship crisis. After all the stunts Caterina pulled, I wanted this weekend to be drama-free. But despite my best efforts, she got the truth out of me. This woman is nothing if not determined.

Last night, over a carton of ice cream and strawberries (ice cream for me, fruit for her, thanks to her returned diet), I confessed the whole sordid story. As expected, she was awesome. She listened when she should, gave advice when asked, and did her hugging thing, which I'm minding less and less. As it turns out, she's of the same opinion as everyone else. That I should call Lucas. It's starting to get to the point where I'm running out of reasons why I haven't.

Jenna's gaze flicks to the mounted clock on the wall. "He still has time to make it here for the reception, you know." She looks back at me, eyebrows furrowed and suddenly very serious-like. "Call. Him."

Stern Jenna is a new sight. For a bride, she's been relatively low-key and blasé—probably a response to finally having Caterina out of her hair. But I'm not aiming to awaken the sleeping bridezilla.

I shift in my seat and fidget with the folds of my dress. It's beautiful. Red silk, figure flattering, it's been hanging in my closet for more than a month. Lucas has drooled over it for just as long. He deserves to see me in this dress.

I roll my eyes at my own ridiculousness. Who am I trying to kid? Dress-shmess, I just want to see him. Be *with* him. Tell him that I loathe space, and time sucks a big one. I know exactly what I want—him. I'm in love with Lucas, and I'm ready for...whatever this is. Long-distance, a few blocks away, whatever it is, I'm in.

It may be too late. He may have to leave anyway. But he's not going anywhere without knowing how I feel.

"Jenna—"

She hands me my phone, which she must've grabbed from the table. "Go outside when you call him," she says with a wink. "Reception is better."

Alessandra squeals as I bolt to my feet, almost knocking out the sweet chica doing my cousin's toenails. "My bad," I holler as every woman in the room waves me out the door.

"Go!" Less's smile is bigger than I've ever seen. Which, for her, is saying something.

"I'm so proud of you." Jenna's smile manages to rival Alessandra's.

For a moment, I stand blinded by how beautiful they are. Then I catch a glimpse of myself in the long mirror behind the chair.

I've never found myself overly attractive. My mouth is bigger than Godzilla. My skin and hair are dull instead of luminescent. I get zits like the rest of the world, and to be honest, I haven't had many reasons, outside of my dad, to smile.

But the girl looking at me is.

Her smile, if it's possible, is even larger than her future mother's or her cousin's. And it doesn't look grotesque. It looks radiant.

Looking into this mirror, I know I'm ready for this next chapter. My heart is full, and it's healed. The only thing missing is the beautiful boy who owns it.

"I'll be right back!"

Rushing down the hall, I wave off Dad and Ransom, lifting my phone in reply to their questions. They probably think I'm insane, but I don't care. I burst through the glass lobby doors and sure enough, instantly get full bars of service. My fingers shake as I click through recent calls and find his name. I take a breath, trying to calm my racing heart so I can actually get words out, and then tap his name.

Ring.

I blow out a puff of air as I begin to pace the manicured sidewalk.

Ring.

"Pick up, Luc. Come on." There's no way he's getting out of this conversation. I'll call his sister, his house, heck, I'll sic Jack on him if I have to.

Ring.

"Greetings and salutations."

My moment of euphoria is dashed by the voice on the other end. I glance at my phone in confusion. "Austin? Why are you answering Lucas's phone?"

They're friends, I guess. It's just that normally if they hang out, we all are. I've never seen the two of them go off and do…whatever it is guy friends do together. And wait, shouldn't Austin be *here*?

"Does Less know where you are?"

"She, in fact, does," he confirms, which immediately makes me suspicious. "Turn around."

I spin in a circle, now utterly confused as I stare at a

parking lot half-filled with cars. A fancy red one pulls in, tires squealing, that looks similar to the one Lucas got hot for in Austin's garage. My eyes narrow and then fly open as I spot two familiar heads through the windshield as the car screeches to a stop in front of me.

"Lucas?" My phone slips from my fingers as he hops out the driver's side door, engine still running. Later, I'll be grateful for my protective phone case, but right now, I couldn't care less. Lucas is *here*.

"Why were you calling me?" he asks, rushing up and pulling me into his arms. "Is something wrong?"

I blink, still completely in shock that this is happening. That he totally hijacked my big moment. Grinning ruefully, I nod. "Yeah, something's wrong. You ruined my grand gesture."

His eyebrows snap together, looking adorably confused, and I laugh. I can't help it. I have no clue why he's here—I'm hoping it's because he misses me as much as I miss him, but either way, I'm taking control of the moment. I don't want to go another second before saying, "Lucas, I love you."

He freezes in place, like he's in shock. In case he is, I decide to say it again.

"I'm in love with you, Lucas. That's why I was calling. To tell you that I'm an idiot for *not* calling and telling you sooner—"

That's as far as I get before his mouth crashes over mine, shushing me. Grinning against his lips, I throw my arms around his neck and hang on tight.

. . .

"You are so beautiful it hurts."

If a heart could burst from being too full, the walls of the elegant Serendipity Ranch ballroom would be splattered with gook. Instead, they are painted a soft cream, a color that seems to glow under the candlelight as Dad twirls Jenna across the floor. As expected, she looks every bit the fairy-tale princess. What is surprising is that I'm in the middle of my own happily ever after in the corner.

Dad interrupted our reunion outside (a situation that wasn't *at all* embarrassing), and ushered us in before Lucas could tell me why he was here. I'm glad; don't get me wrong. But now that the wedding is over, and especially with those sweet, romantic words in my ear, I feel brave enough to ask, "So I didn't ruin this?"

Lucas stares into my eyes and grins. "Do you remember what I told you that night outside of Lyric? When we were out with Alessandra and Austin." He chuckles. "The night she got sloshed and told off a group of bikers?"

I grin at the memory. "They were nothing after those three chicks who were flirting with Austin."

I glance at my cousin snuggling with her man as I think back to the moments *before* we went into the club. When Lucas surprised me by showing up and then giving me a gift that proved he really did see *me,* and not the Hollywood trappings. The night he pretty much said he was coming after me hard.

The night we first kissed.

"Yeah, I remember." I slide my arms around his waist. "You said you weren't going to give up until I told you to." I push to my toes and press a kiss against his lips. Tingles rush over my skin as I pull back and say, "Well, newsflash: that's never gonna happen."

He grins and steals another kiss, one I'm more than eager to give. "Then I guess it's a good thing I'm staying."

I'm skimming my nose along his jaw, breathing in the scent of his cologne mixed with plaster—he must've been working earlier—and marveling at the fact that I almost lost him, so it takes a while for Lucas's words to wiggle through the love-fog. When they do, my eyes pop open.

"What does that mean, exactly?" I'm scared to hope. To jump to conclusions too fast. If he means what I *think* he means, this is now officially the best night of my life. "Is your family staying in the States?"

He exhales and shakes his head regretfully.

"Oh."

My hopes plummet to my shoes.

I guess he meant he's staying with me, as in a long-distance relationship. An outcome I was prepared for. I mean, Milan's not *that* far away. Not with Skype and FaceTime and Instagram. We can do this. And then in two years, I head off to college. Italy must have good schools, right?

Placing a knuckle beneath my chin, Lucas tilts my head up. His fingertips ghost across my cheeks as his palms slide up to cradle my face. "Cat, I'm in love with you." He's said the words already, but I'll never get used to them. "You make me excited to get up in the morning. You challenge me, inspire me, and motivate me. Because of you, a future has opened up that I can't wait to live, and I want you right there beside me as I experience it." His gaze darts to my lips, and he chuckles at what I'm assuming is my dopey grin. "I just hope you don't mind the five-hour commute."

My dopey smile slides away, replaced by a confused

scrunch. *Five hours?* "Come again?"

"The commute from Beverly Hills to San Francisco is five hours," he explains, as if this new, crazy train of thought should make total sense. "Well, according to Google maps it's closer to six, but five sounds better."

He shrugs as he says it, and I mimic the gesture. "Sure, five does sound better." Then I shake my head because it's boggling. "But why am I driving five hours to San Francisco?"

"Oh, did I not mention that?" Lucas's dimples flash as he rests his forehead against mine. "That's where I'll be living."

My breath freezes in my lungs. "What happened to Milan?"

"Cat, you give me something to fight for. I meant it when I said I wasn't going anywhere, that I wasn't giving up until you told me to stay away. On Monday morning, I went to Mr. Scott. He helped me find a boarding school in San Francisco, a school for the arts that is amazing." He glances away, sounding almost dazed as he says, "And they accepted me."

"Of course they accepted you!" I jump up and throw my arms around his neck.

I've actually heard of SFBSA—it's freaking amazing. Lucas wraps me up, laughing as I squeeze him so tight I have to be close to choking off his air supply. "I can't believe this. You're staying." I loosen my hold just enough to lean back and look in his eyes. "You're really staying?"

His chocolate-brown eyes light up as he nods in confirmation. "Dad was a hard sell, but he agreed. Angela and I are staying with Mom until the end of the semester, and then I transfer to SFBSA this summer." He tilts his head and asks, "Do you mind the commute?"

"For you, I'd drive twice that." I shake my head as awe mingles with disbelief. "You fought for me."

My dad loves me unconditionally…but he's my dad. He kind of has to. *Or at least he should*, I think, quickly dismissing thoughts of my vapid mother. Jenna accepts me as her own, and loves me something fierce, but she's an adult. Alessandra, Ransom, Austin—they each care for me, and I know they have my back. But this is different. This is romantic. This is spiritual. This is on another plane.

I chased my birth mother because I needed to feel whole. I needed to know why I wasn't good enough. I was chasing that need in the wrong place. In Lucas's arms, in the way he looks at me and the way he holds me, I have what I was searching for. Here, I feel truly accepted. Here, I feel completely *wanted*.

"Care to dance, maid of honor?"

I smile as I recall the words from the night we met. "*Care to dance, birthday girl?*" Who knew one dance could change everything? It signaled a new beginning for me then, and with what he's told me today, it feels like that again. I slip my hand into his and let Lucas lead me onto the dance floor.

When we reach the center of the room, he slides his hands around my waist and locks them at the small of my back. I run my hands up the soft arms of his Henley, glad that he was in such a rush to get here that he didn't change first. Lucas in sixteenth century garb at my birthday party was hot, and I have no doubt he can rock a suit. But this is him.

Looping my arms around his shoulders, I glance around the room. To my right, Alessandra is dancing with Austin. To my left, Dad is twirling Jenna. And behind me, Hayley is snuggled up with Ransom, looking like the cat that ate the canary. So much about this dance reminds me of our first. Yet so much has changed. *We've* changed. We're stronger now, both individually and together. We have new friends, new relatives, a new and unclear future ahead. But I wouldn't trade a single moment.

The journey isn't over. It's only just beginning. And that rocks.

With a healed heart and completely girlie grin, I rest my head against my boyfriend's chest and close my eyes, letting the feel of my new normal wash over me.

Epilogue: Ciao Bella

·Cat·

Italy hasn't lost its charm. It helps, of course, having my gorgeous boyfriend in tow, but this place will always be special to me. It's where my story began. Seeing it again on the other side, my story not over but a new chapter begun, I feel a sense of accomplishment. Whatever the stars had planned when my gypsy girl came along, I think I did them proud. My new ink proves it.

As it turns out, even with Dad's permission, I couldn't get a second tattoo in California. It's against the law to tattoo minors. But the thought wouldn't let me go. My first one, while done illegally, was a permanent, symbolic reminder of pain. After battling the demons and finding my normal, I wanted a new sign. An image that reflects the girl I am *today*. No longer in hiding, but open to whatever life brings. And totally, utterly, butt-crazy in love.

I place a hand over the ink on my left hip and a smile curves my lips as I lead our group to the Accademia di Belle Arti. Lucas nudges my shoulder. "Still sore?"

"No, just thinking." I glance at him and feign a sigh. "Guess this means I'm stuck with you, huh?"

Laughing, he wraps his arm around my waist. "Better believe it, baby."

Honestly, when I approached Dad and Jenna with the idea for the new tattoo, I didn't think they'd go for it. Have you met my dad? He's the epitome of overprotection. But he surprised me by not only agreeing, but also asking if I had a design in mind. My answer, while dazed, was immediate. I showed them Lucas's sketch from Valentine's Day, the eight-petal rose, and explained its significance. After staring at the paper for a long moment, he pulled me into a hug and kissed the top of my head. His rough, whispered, "I'm proud of you," brought tears to my eyes.

I'm turning into a complete sap.

I spot the doors to the building, and excitement bubbles in my stomach. I pause dramatically before we step inside, meeting everyone's eyes. Dad and Jenna, Ransom and Alessandra, and finally Lucas. "Prepare to be amazed."

We go in, and just like before, students are gathered in groups sketching. This time, I don't wish to join them. Instead, I want to see the look of awe in my loved ones' eyes. The wonder that comes from staring at Michelangelo's masterpiece.

Stopping in front of *David*, the brilliancy of the piece overwhelms me again. Looking down, I catch Alessandra's gaze, and she winks, no doubt remembering when we first saw this together. Five hundred years in the past when the statue was brand new.

The entire trip has been a surreal experience for my cousin, seeing her homeland as it is now. The changes as well as the restoration. She's had moments of sadness for sure, times I've had to distract Dad or make up an excuse for her tears. There's no way he can handle the whole truth just yet. But thankfully, nothing but pure joy radiates from Less's face, and I release a relieved breath.

A few minutes later, a buzzing sounds from my bag. I swing my backpack around, grateful I remembered to quiet my phone. Disturbing the peaceful silence with my rocked-out ringtone would suck. Not to mention be embarrassing. After digging out my cell, I see the name flashing and pull a face.

I'm not in the mood to answer.

Lucas laces our fingers together, not needing to see the screen to know who it is. Tugging me close, he whispers, "Gotta hand it to her. She hasn't given up."

Caterina texted two weeks after our showdown at brunch. It was the coward's way out, texting me an apology instead of calling or even coming by. But she didn't have to do even that. She'd already gotten what she wanted, and from all accounts, her new role revitalized her career. Even so, I ignored her at first. I'd gotten what I needed, too. Closure, a brother, and a way to move on.

But, to my supreme shock, the texts didn't stop.

Another one came the next day, followed by a call that night. They continue even now, a spoken apology and four months later.

Don't get me wrong, I still don't completely trust

Caterina. Half the time we talk, she's as self-involved as ever. But it's the moments where the mask drops, and she's actually *real*, that keep me answering. They're getting more and more frequent. It's possible that one day we'll have the relationship I once hoped for. It's also possible this strained friendship is the best we're going to get.

Either way, I'm good.

My heart no longer has a piece missing. The people around me more than fill that space. I shove my phone in my backpack and rest my head on Lucas's shoulder. After another day here in Florence, we're going to Milan to visit his family. Then it's back to the States, where we'll move Lucas in to his boarding school. The future is wide open and filled with possibility.

And I can't wait to see where it takes me.

Written in the Stars

·Reyna·

From my spot along the wall, I watch as Cat closes her eyes, an expression of peace softening her features. The euphoria that follows fulfilling your destiny.

Since the day she waltzed into my tent almost nine months ago, she has been on a journey. A mission to restore her faith in humanity and to accept the love surrounding her. By escaping to the past, Cat not only gained new relatives, but a fresh perspective. And upon returning, her heart opened to friendship as well as a budding romance.

Watching her now with her family, back where the journey began, I know she is ready for what is to come. She has found her strength and redemption completely in herself. The stars got it right again.

A bittersweet smile curves my lips as I transfer my gaze

to her brother. His journey will be different. Unlike Cat, Ransom is not alone. He has a guide—two actually, counting Alessandra. They have been where he has, traced clues and found their way. Soon, he will be ready to explore the so-called *cryptic* message I once gave him.

Ransom, life is filled with many mysteries. To succeed you must discover your roots and embrace your story. In doing so, you will become the man you were destined to be.

I do not envy his quest. The road set before him will not be easy. Fate never is. But with his sister and cousin standing beside him, my last riddle will not perplex him for long.

Someone bumps me from behind, jostling me from my reverie. The room is quite crowded, especially along the edges where I am spying on my former friends. Turning, I see a young man, perhaps just a tad older than me, eyes bright with apology.

"*Mi scusi.*"

His accent is strong, and his easy smile softens the planes of his chiseled mouth. I watch, flattered, as his gaze subtly scans my attire. Gone is the costume of veils and bangles. As of today, I am no longer a servant of the stars. For the first time—in a very *long* time—I am simply me. Reyna Puceanu.

A woman who has her *own* life to lead.

"No apology necessary," I say, pushing my shoulder away from the wall. "Enjoy the art."

The man opens his mouth, as if to entice me to stay, and I smile as I walk away. Romance is not in the cards for me today… but soon. Cat, Alessandra, and Ransom have one another now. My assignment is complete. With one last glance at the friends I have made this last year, I exhale and step out into the bright, Florentine sunshine, and walk toward my future.

Toward *my* destiny.

Acknowledgments

Now we've come to my favorite section of any book — where you get to see the author get all misty-eyed over everyone who helped make her latest story a reality. It never ceases to amaze me how many people are truly involved in the creative process. Writing at your computer can be isolating, but publishing is far from it. To everyone who had a hand in making this story a reality, thank you.

Ashley Bodette, thank you for brainstorming and answering a bazillion and a half what if questions with me. For reading my scary outlines and going over the same scenes until they're perfect...thank you. You are a blessing and the best assistant ever, and I don't know how I would've gotten through the last year without you holding my hand. You have a friend for life, chica.

Without guidance from Ashley, Trisha Wolfe, Shannon Duffy, Caisey Quinn, Mindy Ruiz, Michelle Madow, Mary Hinson, Heather Self, and Kayleigh Gore, this book probably wouldn't exist. I'd be stuck in my head and still staring at a blinking cursor. These girls kept me writing, kept me inspired, and they made the entire process a joy. They critiqued and beta-read my drafts, gave fabulous feedback, drove around LAX with their camera phones so I can see it (love ya, Mindy!), and truly got my characters and the story I wanted to tell. Love you, girls!

It's not possible to go through this without a handful of dear friends who understand your crazy. Who provide emotional support, laughter, handholding, advice, and so much more than I can even name here. Cindi Madsen, Melissa West, Tara Fuller, Lisa Burstein, Meagan Erickson, Christina Lee, Stina Lindenblatt, Rhonda Helms, Wendy Higgins, and Cole Gibsen, you girls are my mafia. I love you to pieces, and all of you are "cool" and "foxy" in my eyes. ;)

Stacy Abrams is my literary fairy godmother. She polished my words until they shined, humored my quirky freak-outs, and loved these characters as much as I do. She asked for even more from their worlds and provided a safe, fun, supportive atmosphere with Entangled. She kept me laughing through the edits and made me sound so much smarter than I am. *mwah*

My street team, the Flirt Squad, is seriously the best support team ever. They keep me smiling. They support me AND each other. They offer fabulous advice and laugh with me whenever I "pull a Rachel." Girls, thank you so much for the love, the laughs, the ideas, and most importantly, the friendship. You make this journey a blast. I'm the luckiest author ever, and I heart you all. An extra special shout-out to member Holly Underhill, who won a contest and became a character—I hope you had a blast living in Cat's crazy

world! And Shelley Bunnell, thanks for naming Ransom—
he turned out to be one of my favorite characters. Hope he
didn't remind you too much of your dog (tee hee)

I couldn't possibly thank every team member. Each
and every one of them makes me smile, do a giddy dance,
and cry happy tears. But a few rock stars in particular
went WAY beyond leading up to this release, so Saleana
Carneiro, Meredith Johnson, Jen Stasi, Veronica Bartles,
Cindy Hale, Crystal Leach, Valerie Fink, Jessica Mangicaro,
Staci Murden, Zoe Miller, Kathy Arugelles, Shelley Bunnell,
Katrina Tinnon, and Heather Love King, consider yourselves
virtually tackle hugged.

Debbie Suzuki and Jamie Arnold, thank you for leading
up the tour and for your constant support. Kelly Simmon
of InkSlinger PR, you rock my world. Damaris Carinali
of Good Choice Reading, Christine of I*Heart*BigBooks
(and I cannot lie...), and E.M. Tippetts, you are all simply
amazing. Thank you for your talent, your friendship, and
your support. Love, love, so much love.

Chris and Michelle Holmes, thank you for putting up
with my random, plentiful questions about all things "car"
and "mechanical." For the links to cool videos, the inside
intel, and for totally inspiring a future book idea during our
chats — YOU ROCK!

This series found an enthusiastic audience and from
book one, I've gotten questions about Cat and Lucas. I hope
this story lived up to your hopes and answered most of your
questions. Who knows, there may be more fun to come.
Thank you for loving these characters so fiercely!

And finally, my family. They deserve so much more than a
measly paragraph, but they know how lost I would be without

them. My daughters, Jordan and Cali, are my number-one fans, and they are why I do this. I hope they see that anything is possible, and if you chase a dream hard enough, you can make it happen. Mama loves you girls. It's an honor to be your mother and your teacher, and the memories we make each day in our homeschool inspire the words that I write. My mother-in-law, Peggy, reads every book I write, and isn't shy about making sure everyone knows about them. I love that—and I love her! My parents, Rosie and Ronnie, and my brother, Ryan, give me amazing feedback, constant support, and free babysitting. They are the best cheerleaders ever, and I love them so, so much. And finally, my husband, Gregg, is my rock. His faith is unbelievable, his love too awesome to comprehend, and his encouragement such a blessing. He is the reason I know true love exists, and he inspires every love story I tell. SHMILY, baby!!

About the Author

As a teen, Rachel Harris threw raging parties that shook her parents' walls and created embarrassing fodder for future YA novels. As an adult, she reads and writes obsessively, rehashes said embarrassing fodder, and dreams up characters who become her own grownup versions of imaginary friends.

When not typing furiously or flipping pages in an enthralling romance, she homeschools her two beautiful girls and watches too much reality television with her amazing husband. She writes young adult, new adult, and adult Fun & Flirty Escapes, including *My Super Sweet Sixteenth Century*, *A Tale of Two Centuries*, and her adult romances *Taste the Heat* and *Seven Day Fiancé*. Rachel LOVES talking with readers! Find her at: RachelHarrisWrites.com.

Sign up for our Steals & Deals newsletter and be the first to hear about 99¢ releases from Rachel Harris and other fantastic Entangled authors!

Reviews help other readers find books. We appreciate all reviews, whether positive or negative. Thank you for reading!

Other books by Rachel Harris...

MY SUPER SWEET SIXTEENTH CENTURY

On the precipice of her sixteenth birthday, the last thing lone wolf Cat Crawford wants is an extravagant gala thrown by her bubbly stepmother and well-meaning father. So even though Cat knows the family's trip to Florence, Italy, is a peace offering, she embraces the magical city and all it offers. But when her curiosity leads her to an unusual gypsy tent, she exits...right into Renaissance Firenze.

Thrust into the sixteenth century armed with only a backpack full of contraband future items, Cat joins up with her ancestors, the sweet Alessandra and protective Cipriano, and soon falls for the gorgeous aspiring artist Lorenzo. But when the much-older Niccolo starts sniffing around, Cat realizes that an unwanted birthday party is nothing compared to an unwanted suitor full of creeptastic amore. Can she find her way back to modern times before her Italian adventure turns into an Italian forever?

A TALE OF TWO CENTURIES

Alessandra D'Angeli is in need of an adventure. Tired of her sixteenth-century life in Italy and homesick for her time-traveling cousin, Cat, who visited her for a magical week and dazzled her with tales of the future, Alessandra is lost. Until the stars hear her plea.

One mystical spell later, Alessandra appears on Cat's Beverly Hills doorstep five hundred years in the future. Surrounded by confusing gadgets, scary transportation, and scandalous clothing, Less is hesitant to live the life of a twenty-first century teen...until she meets the infuriating—and infuriatingly handsome—surfer Austin Michaels. Austin challenges everything she believes in…and introduces her to a world filled with possibility.

With the clock ticking, Less knows she must live every moment of her modern life while she still can. But how will she return to the drab life of her past when the future is what holds everything she's come to love?

For adult readers…

Taste the Heat

When chef Colby Robicheaux returned home to New Orleans to save her family restaurant, the last person she expected to reconnect with was her brother's best friend and her childhood crush. As tempting as a sugar-coated beignet, Jason is one dish she doesn't want to taste. Colby is counting down the days till she can leave the place where her distrust of love and commitment originated and go back to Vegas.

Fire captain Jason Landry isn't looking for love, either. He knows he should focus on finding the perfect mother for his daughter, but when he first sees Colby, all grown up and gorgeous, he can't help but be drawn to her. And when she suggests a no-strings-attached fling, Jason doesn't want to say no.

As their relationship grows more intense, Colby finds that Jason isn't as easy to leave behind as she thought. Could turning up the heat on something real be worth the possibility of getting burned?

Seven Day Fiancé

Angelle Prejean is in a pickle. Her family is expecting her to come home with a fiancé—a fiancé who doesn't exist. Well, he exists, but he definitely has no idea Angelle told her mama they were engaged. Tattooed, muscled, and hotter than sin, Cane can reduce Angelle to a hot mess with one look—and leave her heart a mess if she falls for him. But when she ends up winning Cane at a charity bachelor auction, she knows just how to solve her fiancé problem.

Cane Robicheaux is no one's prince. He doesn't do relationships and he doesn't fall in love. When sweet, sultry-voiced Angelle propositions him, he hopes their little game can finally get her out of his head. He doesn't expect her to break through all his barriers. But even as Angelle burrows deeper into his heart, he knows once their seven days are up, so is their ruse.

Check out Entangled's new teen releases...

FRAGILE LINE
by Brooklyn Skye

It can happen in a flash. One minute she's kissing her boyfriend, the next she's lost in the woods. Sixteen-year-old Ellie Cox is losing time. It started out small...forgetting a drive home or a conversation with a friend. But her blackouts are getting worse, more difficult to disguise as forgetfulness. When Ellie goes missing for three days, waking up in the apartment of a mysterious guy—a guy who is definitely not her boyfriend— her life starts to spiral out of control.

Perched on the edge of insanity, with horrific memories of her childhood leaking in, Ellie struggles to put together the pieces of what she's lost—starting with the name haunting her, Gwen. Heartbreakingly beautiful and intimately drawn, this poignant story follows one girl's harrowing journey to finding out who she really is.

WHERE YOU'LL FIND ME
by Erin Fletcher

When Hanley Helton discovers a boy living in her garage, she knows she should kick him out. But Nate is too charming to be dangerous. He just needs a place to get away, which Hanley understands. Her own escape methods—vodka, black hair dye, and pretending the past didn't happen—are more traditional, but who is she to judge?

Nate doesn't tell her why he's in her garage, and she doesn't tell him what she's running from. Soon, Hanley¹s trading her late night escapades for all-night conversations and stolen kisses. But when Nate¹s recognized as the missing teen from the news, Hanley isn't sure which is worse: that she's harboring a fugitive, or that she's in love with one.

SEARCHING FOR BEAUTIFUL
by Nyrae Dawn

Before it happened…

Brynn had a group of best friends, a boyfriend who loved her, a growing talent for pottery. She had a life. And then…she had none.

After it happened…

Everything was lost. The boy she now knew never loved her. The friends who felt she betrayed their trust. The new life just beginning to grow inside her.

Brynn believes her future is as empty as her body until Christian, the boy next door, starts coming around. Playing his guitar and pushing her to create art once more. She meets some new friends at the local community center, plus even gets her dad to look her in the eye again…sort of. But letting someone in isn't as easy as it seems.

Now…

Can Brynn open up her heart to truly find her life's own beauty, when living for the after means letting go of the before?

CPSIA information can be obtained at www.ICGtesting.com
Printed in the USA
LVOW10s1125280516

490363LV00010B/189/P

9 781500 552732